KARUNA RIAZI

A Bit of Earth

Greenwillow Books

An Imprint of HarperCollins*Publishers*

A Bit of Earth

All rights reserved. No part of this book may be used or reproduced in any manner whatsoever without written permission except in the case of brief quotations embodied in critical articles and reviews. Printed in the United States of America. For information address HarperCollins Children's Books, a division of HarperCollins Publishers, 195 Broadway, New York, NY 10007.
www.harpercollinschildrens.com

The text of this book is set in Adobe Thai.
Book design by Sylvie Le Floc'h

Library of Congress Control Number: 2022952417
ISBN 9780063098664 (hardcover)

23 24 25 26 27 LBC 5 4 3 2 1
First Edition
Greenwillow Books

*To all the Marias out there, looking for their special,
safe bit of earth in this world.
May you find it, so that you are able to not just survive—
but thrive. May you be nourished, and supported,
and loved, for all that you are.
May you be able to bloom into all your bright
and beautiful potential.*

A Bit of Earth

I *· Arrivals*

Maria never felt comfortable in
airports.

Never mind that she knew how to hide it,
as surely as any traveler would.

Take out any keys
have their passport open
be ready to lift their backpack onto the belt
step through the scanner please.

Maria didn't feel comfortable anywhere.

But airports were particularly awful.

The sight of a terminal made her stomach clench,
her feet falter.

Security was a nightmare.

(Security would always be a nightmare
when you were

brown skinned
and brown eyed
and your dupatta
so threadbare and worn through
was still too thick for a heavy-handed agent
to see your hair instead of a
knife

or

grenade.)

Security.

Se-cur-i-ty.

That was a word that meant

standing upward, arms spread

and then down

and then, move on.

No rest or ease
for a girl like her.

No chance to
put down roots
and grow.

Security was not a word for Maria's vocabulary.
As it turns out, when you were always
arriving
you were never actually
leaving.
You never got a chance to stay.

One

There were two good reasons why Maria didn't respond when she heard the announcement over the airport terminal intercom.

The first reason was the announcement itself: "Attention, please, this is gate B32 calling for a passenger who was on flight 6789, arriving from Islamabad with connections in Dubai and Brussels. Passenger Mary Latif, please report to the nearest information desk or meet your party at carousel eleven in the baggage claim area. Passenger Mary Latif, please report . . ."

Considering that her name wasn't Mary, she felt pretty confident about not turning up to the nearest information desk or meeting her party.

If they weren't careful with a name, what would they do with an unattended kid?

And the second, which was more significant, was this:

Maria did not want to be found.

This would probably be deemed unpleasant behavior by any adult. Especially given that Maria knew she was being searched for by two frantic women, one of whom was worried she might lose her job.

And those adults would be right. Even Maria would admit to it.

She was unpleasant.

There was no one more unpleasant in that airport at that moment in time than Maria.

Well, probably.

She'd walked off the plane past the McDonald's line, after all, and there was always some child having a meltdown over the Happy Meal toy and making the adult with them regret their life choices.

That child, and the unending noise of terminal four, despite it being barely four in the morning, was part of why Maria was here, in the very corner of the baggage claim area with a heap of unclaimed luggage around her.

It wasn't like she was grabbing people's bags from under them. If they were here without owners, well, they were free for use.

So she was using them, to make a tower of solitude.

And ignoring the two women, not all that far away, panicked about where she was. Because she was unpleasant.

Maria had also heard the words "hostile," "ungrateful," and "nasty," in the year since her parents died. Ambreen Phuppo, her father's half-sister, liked to sum Maria's attitude up in one quick, angry match strike of Urdu: "Maria! Badtameez."

Which is "unpleasant," "ungrateful" and "nasty," bundled up with an extra pinch of guilt and a jab at your bad manners.

Maria didn't mind. Bad manners kept her sharp. She didn't want her aunt to think she actually *liked* her bossy and clingy nature—and when Phuppo washed her hands of Maria and shipped her off to America, it had only confirmed Maria's approach to life. Badtameez girls were girls who didn't get hurt.

Even hidden as she was beneath duffel bags, wheelies, and one or two large suitcases, Maria snapped to attention at the sound of her name.

Or at least something close to it.

"Yes, her name's Maria," a woman said.

The breathless voice definitely didn't belong to Yusra, the weary cousin of a cousin several hundred times removed, who probably regretted promising to chaperone Maria to New York on her way to rejoin her husband in Milwaukee.

Yusra would say her name right: *Mah*-ri-a. Quick. Clever. Unpleasant, when you made it too sharp. Like her.

Not Ma-*rhee*-ah: dragged out like a lazy, sticky piece of gum.

So it had to be the lady from the alumni organization. Gillian the liaison, or something like that. It sounded like an unpleasant bump, the kind Maria got on her tongue from green mangos or hard candy—both things she hated more than anything else.

But it suited the lady, with her white pantsuit, long blond braid, and smile frozen as neatly as if she were a newscaster in a paused recording.

Maria couldn't remember the name of the organization, but it had something to do with where her parents had gone to college and the circle of lawyers and fellow activist types they'd been friends with.

Maria scowled.

It was the alumni organization's fault that she was here, in New York City, the last place on Earth she ever wanted to be.

She was their latest charity case.

"They want you to have better opportunities, beta," her Ambreen Phuppo had explained, anxiously wringing her hands. "They didn't know their friends' daughter was having such a hard time finding a place to stay."

"But I'm with you now," Maria said.

Phuppo and her husband, Hassan Phuppa, exchanged glances. Maria could read them, even though they thought she couldn't: *Well, we don't want you here.*

She knew that she was dour faced and thin, that she scowled in every family picture, and that even her beautiful, cool older cousins had shrugged and given up after the third time she rolled over and went to sleep during a "sister bonding sleepover."

It didn't hurt to think it, or accept it. She was prickly, after all. And she liked it that way.

What she didn't like, though, was not being left to her own prickly devices in Pakistan or with her mother's family in Bangladesh, but instead being shipped off to America because her parents' old friends thought she needed "all the opportunities her parents would have wanted her to have."

And if there was anything Maria was most tired of— something she was always told was ungrateful to think or say out loud—it was everyone telling her what her parents would have wanted for her.

Even she didn't know what her parents wanted for her. They had been gone so often.

And now they were gone for good.

Maria swallowed hard against the sudden knot in her

throat and pushed another suitcase firmly into place. She wasn't going to stay in here forever. How could she? But right now it was nice, and quiet.

Warm. Secure.

All the things she had rarely felt since that call in the middle of the night, and the news that her parents wouldn't be coming back from their trip.

And the best part was that Yusra and Gillian the liaison weren't in here with her. Yusra had been tolerable once she figured out that the best way to avoid Maria's unpleasantness was not to interact with her.

But Gillian—there was something about the way she'd stared at Maria, eyes welling up in spite of the dry terminal air.

"You look so much like your mom," she sniffed.

Maria knew she absolutely did not, but she muttered thank you and shifted behind Yusra as quickly as she could.

It wasn't just grief in Gillian's eyes. It was hunger.

Many people are like Gillian. They are not bad people. They look at the world where it has been carefully cleaned and tucked behind their computer screen and think, *This is all I need to know.*

These people do not ask questions about kids like Maria. Questions such as:

"Do these children want to be cuddled and cooed at

like they are animals, and not actual people who understand English?"

"What brought them here, to this airport?"

"Do they want to be here?"

Of course Maria did not want to be cuddled or cooed at like some poor unfortunate soul. And New York City was the last place on Earth she had expected any of her relatives to send her.

Looking at Maria and thinking of her as a pathetic character in an infomercial wasn't just ridiculous.

It was a mistake.

One that Gillian wouldn't be making again. At least, once she realized she'd made it. When it came to Maria, everyone had to learn the hard way.

"Give us just a minute, and stay right here," Gillian had said, after Yusra had escorted Maria to the meeting point in the baggage area.

Maria nodded. "Right here."

Yusra gave her a suspicious look. Maria gazed innocently back. But it was true.

Just not entirely the way that Gillian thought.

Gillian meant, "Here, in our sight."

Maria meant, "Here, in terminal four of JFK, and possibly in this same area if I feel like it."

Gillian and Yusra hunched over a sheaf of papers, shuffling and whispering as they slid pages out to be signed, then back into the stack.

Then she heard one sentence escape from behind Yusra's cupped, red-nail-bearing hand.

"She was just so unpleasant, I didn't know what to do with her."

It was a good thing Maria knew exactly what to do with herself.

She'd quickly found the coziest spot: two carousels down, among the stacks of unclaimed luggage.

Gillian's voice rang out, strained and urgent.

"Can you just page her again, please?"

"Ma'am, please give me some space." Another voice came distantly, accompanied by the snap-crackle-pop of a walkie-talkie. "Does the little girl speak any English?"

"Enough. A little. I don't know."

Maria bit her tongue and rolled her eyes.

If there was anything Maria had enough of in both pockets, it was words.

She'd forced her way into the front row of every class she had attended in her short life: first at the modest-sized madrasah, and then evening classes in the small masjid, when they lived in Switzerland long enough for her to be enrolled.

She clung to those memories hungrily, as much as the Kashmiri words that lined the bottom of her pocket. On top of that, she'd scattered Urdu from the conversations and complaints hissed over her head, Bengali from her mother and her family, a bit of Arabic from her father's friends, enough Farsi to warm both hands—

And even though her parents had never brought her back more than a few unfamiliar chocolate brands from their overseas excursions, Maria Latif knew English.

"She can't have gotten far," Yusra said. She sounded harried. Her connecting flight was coming up. Otherwise, she probably wouldn't have cared if her troublesome not-quite-a-cousin got lost in the Big Apple. "Don't you have anyone who could help us search the area? She's a child. Anything could happen."

Maria sighed, feeling the bags sag with her.

Sooner or later, that security guard would weary enough of the fussing to take a good look, and then she would be discovered.

And it would be over.

The brief bit of freedom in between being firmly watched.

Warm air wafted over Maria's nose, and she froze.

The air in the terminal was cold, not warm. It stung when it smacked against her face. And it was thick with strong odors.

She inhaled brief glimpses of other people's lives through the aromas that clung to the carpet and on their bags: mint toothpaste, sharply alcoholic perfume, and salted peanuts from the flight.

But this new air was soft. Mild. It smelled like sunshine through an open window, like fragrant spices from a neighbor's house, like flowers being brushed up against and kindly exhaling their scent.

It smelled fresher than anything in a major airport should.

Maria closed her eyes and swayed slightly as a strange feeling rolled down her neck.

It tickled the hair on the back of her arms like a ray of sunlight.

It glided over her feet, sticky and stiff in shoes a distant cousin had already molded.

It itched like new grass.

Something, somewhere in this new place, coaxed her to put down her bag. Asked her to take root.

But why? What was happening to her?

Maria opened her eyes, and gasped.

Someone stared in at her, through the gaps between the luggage. Then she saw a raised hand—fingers reaching toward the suitcase above her.

Maria shifted back. That was a mistake.

Maria was born prickly, she was sure. Even her bones had sharp little spurs at the end, preparing for her to toss out her elbows and squat, unmovable and stony faced, in doorways for people to trip over and fume at.

And now, her bony elbow jutted into another suitcase. The entire tower of solitude collapsed.

Maria threw up her hands to shield her face. When the commotion settled, she slowly lowered them—to the sight of surprised expressions all around her:

A security guard nearby, round and red cheeked, raising a walkie-talkie to his mouth.

Yusra, shaking her head, already stepping forward to drag Maria to her feet.

Gillian, hand flying to her mouth, eyes wide and horrified.

And another woman, a new woman, still holding the red duffel bag that she had pulled out from the tower, staring at Maria.

It was, even for Maria, a very unpleasant sequence of events.

II ✎ *Maria*
A Testimony (or Two)

Phuppo, a *loving aunt*
        (she says)
the closest relative the poor child has
        (yes, close, Maria would agree)
        (as close to irritated skin as a hangnail).
She sticks out like a sore thumb,
doesn't she,
among my girls?
        (Yes, Maria takes pleasure
        in nursing the constant ache
        of sticking out in an otherwise content
        finger family: of being
        different
        and sullen.)
It doesn't matter how much rice I keep aside for her.
Nothing sticks to her bones.
She always has that
angry hunger
clinging to her cheeks and in her eyes.
        (What use is rice
        when you need to swallow it

with an eye on the clock

and another on your bags waiting at the door?)

Maria was used to it.

A relative will say,

Of course

let her stay with me.

Chide her for looking too often at the time.

You can be here as long as you like.

And then

after one day

or perhaps two

their gaze is

right there

on the moving hands with her.

Not that it bothers Maria:

darkening a doorway,

never quite letting your feet

learn the pathway

through it.

But it doesn't help.

> (Neither does Phuppo's rice having the
> consistency of a stirred-up riverbed:
> soggy leaves, aging fish, and mud.)

A relative who could only keep Maria a few weeks
wishes her all the best
as long as it is away from her.
I worry about how fierce she looks.
How she doesn't cast her eyes to the ground.
A child like that, those with bad intentions like to single
them out . . .
taunt them, ask where their fathers are.
Of course
I don't want them to.

> (Of course
> you do.
> Of course Maria knew
> she was a child that adults—
> guiltily
> maybe—
> wanted to see life shake by the shoulders
> hold upside down

until the blood rushed to her head
and in her ears
and her stomach flopped about.)

One relative,
or maybe them all
      (in between car windows
      during hushed phone calls
      clustered in rows in the aftermath
      of the cold, quiet janazah).
If only she had her mother's spirit.
If only she had her father's smile.
If only they had taken their
beautiful
gleaming
star-bright
faces into her room more often than they did,
let her absorb their glow
so when the time came she could generate her own,
perhaps she wouldn't be this way.

What way?

Cold.

Distant.
Never happy.

She's just so
unpleasant.

> (She knows that too.
> And she prefers it that way.
> Better to be quiet
>> sullen
>> Maria Latif
> poking at flower beds and
> dragging books out of
> fellow students' hands
> than to be meek
>> round cheeked
>> squirming
>> and
>> trampled underfoot
>> before she even had a chance
> to sprout.)

Two

"Maria! What were you thinking?"

Yusra's cheeks were flushed as she leaned down, brushing off the knees of Maria's shalwar pants. Maria didn't bother to tell her that the stains were likely not from the terminal floor. Most of her outfits these days were years old, passed down from a cousin who hadn't taken the best care with them.

"If your aunt could see you like this . . . ," Yusra continued, but Maria tuned her out.

Her eyes were fixed on the woman who'd nearly been buried by her protective tower, now standing quietly next to Gillian with no expression, hands clasped behind her back.

She shouldn't be so interesting to look at, considering how flat and pale and ordinary she was: long black hair pulled back in a ponytail, black knit beanie, and long brown trench coat, big boots.

There was something about her, though, hovering like perfume, beckoning Maria closer.

Maria took a step away from Yusra, but her escort reached out and grasped her shoulders. Her lips were thin.

"Oh no you don't. Not again." She looked at the closest security guard. "I'm so sorry about this."

The man shook his head, his expression showing that he didn't want to get involved but also that he very much sympathized with her.

Maria rolled her eyes.

No one had rushed forward to claim the fallen luggage yet.

This was why she couldn't stand grown-ups. They made such a big deal of everything.

"Yusra," Gillian chirruped. "In all this commotion, I wasn't able to let you know Lyndsay was coming. I'm so sorry about that."

Yusra turned to Gillian and the woman still hanging back behind her. Her brow furrowed.

"Lyndsay?"

"Clayborne," the woman—Lyndsay—offered, extending her hand.

Yusra shook it cautiously, her eyes narrowed.

"As in Ethan Clayborne? My cousin's husband's roommate?"

It was amazing how Bangladeshi aunties kept such complicated associations in their heads.

"Yes," Lyndsay said, her face animating just a bit. "My husband."

"Husband? But . . . I thought that was Saira?"

Yusra was looking suspicious again, until Gillian leaned in, her face flush with embarrassment.

"Saira . . . passed away, remember? Lyndsay is the second Mrs. Clayborne."

"Oh. Oh!" Now Yusra flushed. "I'm so sorry. . . ."

Lyndsay waved it off, but Maria was watching her face. Something had passed through her eyes when Gillian mentioned her being the second Mrs. Clayborne. She wasn't sure what it was—pain? resignation? jealousy?—but she filed it away for future consideration.

"Yusra," Gillian continued. "Lyndsay has stepped in for Asra."

"Stepped in for . . . is Asra Apu not coming?"

"As I'm sure you know, Asra's mother is very ill—"

"Yes, I do know, as they are related to me," Yusra broke in irritably. "What about it?"

"Well." Gillian fidgeted. "I'm so sorry, she tried to call you, but you were in the air, you see. Asra had to leave, very unexpectedly, for South Africa. Her mother took a turn for the worse. She won't be back for a few weeks at least."

Maria was suddenly more interested in the conversation. Asra was the other distant cousin who'd been charged with taking on the problem that was Maria Latif.

If Asra wasn't coming, would Maria be sent back to Lahore?

Hope sparked in her chest. It wasn't like she wanted to be back under Phuppo's watchful eye, but the thought of escaping New York City . . .

"I thought . . ." Yusra seemed utterly taken aback. "We did discuss that she might have to leave, but she assured us Maria could go with her."

Maria glanced at her sharply.

What?

No one had told her anything like that. What about Phuppo's long lecture two nights ago, insisting that she would have so much opportunity in America, and that was why they were sending her away?

The grown-ups were still talking over her head.

"The amount of red tape to take a . . . well, unhoused orphan child with her . . . ," Gillian was murmuring.

Yusra's face was grim. "So what am I supposed to do with her? I can't possibly take her when my in-laws are only expecting me. I have to call Ambreen—"

"There's no need for that," Gillian interrupted. "We sent an email through the alumni list service to see if anyone else was willing to be . . . well, a halfway house of sorts for the time being. We had so many kind offers, but when Asra and I saw Ethan Clayborne's name, we knew he'd be the right person for Maria to stay with. He and Maria's father were so close, after all, in their college days."

"But it was so long ago," Yusra protested. "And Mr. Clayborne . . ."

"Is away temporarily on business, but he is invested in Maria's safety and wants to honor his friendship with Mahmood," Lyndsay said smoothly. It sounded too rehearsed to Maria, but Yusra's shoulders lowered a bit.

Especially when she added, "I promise that my mother-in-law and I will make sure Maria is comfortable and safe during her time here. Asra and I are close too, so we'll be in touch. I know it'll work out."

But there was something about the way she delivered it all—as smooth and flat as her face and hair—that Maria didn't like.

"I want to go back to Pakistan." Maria broke into the

conversation. "Or Bangladesh. My naanu's family said they would take me in."

"Maria, you know your grandmother can't care for you anymore," Yusra said impatiently. "Wait a moment, please."

She looked between Lyndsay and Gillian, her brows furrowed.

"The alumni organization has already made sure we'll take care of any expenses for Maria's time here, so no need to work about that," Gillian cooed, her face anxious.

"The alumni organization doesn't have to do anything for me," Maria insisted, stamping her foot. "I don't want to be here. I was enrolled in school in Pakistan. I got pulled out. Let me just go and I can come back when Asra Apu is ready for me."

But it seemed the decision was out of Maria's hands.

Yusra turned to Lyndsay Clayborne.

"Take care of her, please," she said.

Lyndsay nodded. But she didn't look confident.

Maria's stomach sank.

III ✒ Constellations

Maria's parents were
celestial bodies
for as long as she could remember.

New York.
Los Angeles.
London.
Paris.

Those were the names of
their galaxies:
the spangled shimmering cities
they orbited
like small moons
wistfully gathering the glow
from a more impressive sun.

Maria remembered, one evening,
the yearning twang of the rabab
like birdsong filtering through open window shutters
the crackling radio
and

her beautiful starlit mother

cradling her head in her hand

murmuring street names, dreamily, like they were a supplication:

"Canal Street. Avenue of the Americas. *Broadway.*"

Maria hated them all.

Those cities had their own sacred glow

but drew in her parents too, to add to their light,

and she was left behind

to live on smaller planets

where old mattresses stamped their dark grievances into her spine

in Bangladesh

or Pakistan

(which she hated—or thought she had—

of course she did—

how could she not?)

Better not to live in a constellation where she did not belong.

Better not to be in a city where they would have felt

safe
luminous
at home . . .
and she, a lesser star, never would.

Three

Stepping outside an airport terminal before dawn was more a vivid dream than something Maria was actually experiencing.

She blinked as the chill wind whipped across her cheeks, bringing strong and lingering smells that were both familiar and foreign to her nose: damp asphalt, traces of a passing woman's floral perfume, and car exhaust.

A cacophony of car horns, raised voices, and clattering shoes surrounded her. Families hustled to impatient taxis, carting sleepy children in their arms and trying to force strollers into trunks that looked tinier than Maria's own suitcase. Swarming TSA workers in bright orange jackets tapped on idling car windows and huddled in corners to murmur quietly. One turned to her, his gaze hard, and

Maria quickly looked away, focusing on her breath making little cold clouds in front of her nose.

She had expected New York to be bright. But it was dingy, more cluttered, and more litter strewn than anywhere else she'd been.

Maria cast a furtive look at her new guardian. Lyndsay Clayborne was deep in conversation with Gillian. Or at least, that was what Maria thought was happening, considering how hard Gillian's head was bobbing up and down. Lyndsay was turned away from Maria completely, not even her shoulders rising and falling to indicate what she might be saying.

If she was saying anything at all.

She hadn't said much as they walked Yusra back to the security checkpoint. It didn't bother Maria, not really. The blank expression that didn't give away anything did, though.

Yusra kept frowning at Lyndsay, taking in her long trench coat and tugged-down knit hat. Maria almost rolled her eyes. She wasn't sure why she was making a show and dance of worrying about Maria when, up until this point, Yusra had seemed quite ready to wash her hands of her very distantly related and bothersome cargo.

Once they reached the checkpoint, she turned to Maria and said, "Be good, baba, all right? I gave you my number in Milwaukee, so call whenever, okay?"

Maria nodded. Yusra had given Maria her number early in their flight from Dubai, when she was still full of the engaged tell-me-about-yourself attitude all grown-ups had at first.

When Yusra had dozed off during the in-flight movie, Maria quietly excused herself to the bathroom and lost it in the trash can.

She didn't think Yusra would mind.

Yusra gave Lyndsay one more look, and Gillian a tight smile.

And then she was gone.

Gillian looked down at Maria, patting her on the shoulder with that million-watt smile firmly in place.

"You doing okay there, kiddo?"

Obviously there was guidance given by the organization to make sure the fragile orphan didn't have an embarrassing emotional meltdown in the middle of the airport. What did they think they were dealing with, a chick right out of the egg?

Maria looked back up, making sure to put on her most unimpressed there's-not-even-an-itch-at-the-corners-of-my-eyes stare.

Phuppo called it the dadima look.

It was just as effective for Maria as for any grandmother. Gillian took her hand right off and busied herself with talking to Lyndsay from then on.

Now she stopped on the sidewalk, keys in her hands.

"Give Mr. Clayborne my regards." Gillian directed this over her head to Lyndsay. There was, suddenly, an awkward look on her face. The same look Maria's elder cousins got when they mentioned their own parents in front of Maria, like the orphan was going to crumble because other people still got to have those.

"We're all glad," Gillian suddenly rushed out. "You know, that you two . . . that you and him . . . well . . ."

She trailed off, hands darting about in the air. But something flared in Lyndsay's face. Maria couldn't explain it, but it looked almost like Lyndsay was, finally, feeling something.

And it wasn't a good something.

"Thanks," Lyndsay said, with a tight smile.

Gillian glanced down at Maria, as though finally remembering there was an audience for her little display. Maria gazed back.

"Take care, you two," she chirruped, and darted toward a taxi with her hand raised.

"Thank god," Lyndsay muttered.

Maria's head jerked up, and she stared at the woman. Had she really just . . .

But then the crosswalk light changed. Lyndsay strode forward.

Maria grasped her suitcase handle and plunged after her.

She'd been on more hectic roads in a million other places, but in spite of herself, her breath came fast and she scrambled to keep up with Lyndsay's long strides.

How had the street looked so small when they were standing at the edge, but was so wide now?

Maria tried to square her shoulders, hyper aware of her raggedy bag and squeaky wheels bouncing on each and every crack in the pavement.

She didn't even notice when the light changed.

"Hey, what are you doing, honey?"

A firm hand on her elbow dragged her from the crosswalk to a pavement island as an angry car blared out a warning.

Maria blinked, watching as several cars zoomed past where she'd been standing. A woman stood over her, a thin frown creasing her lips.

"You gotta be careful, all right?"

Aw-right? It sounded like she was chewing her words. Maria had to play them back twice in her head, mentally running her fingers over the accent.

"Maria?" Lyndsay rushed back, car keys grasped in her hand. "What happened?"

The woman turned to her. "She almost got run over. You need to pay more attention, okay? Moms these days."

"Oh, I . . ." Lyndsay glanced between Maria and the woman. "I'm sorry." She reached out for Maria's suitcase. "Come on, let's go. The car is over there."

Maria glanced back, hoping the stranger would say something else in that intriguing accent. But the woman just shook her head again and walked briskly in the opposite direction.

Lyndsay still hadn't slowed down. Her eyes were on her hands, which—Maria realized—didn't just hold her keys, but a cell phone.

Was she expecting a call? Who would be calling at this hour?

Could she already be willing Gillian to reappear and say that Asra could actually take Maria in after all? If that was the case, maybe they had more in common than Maria thought.

Hah. As if.

No. The firm rule for dealing with adults, particularly ones not related to her, was *Don't expect anything from them.*

Like, at all.

Ever.

Lyndsay Clayborne was a substitute for a substitute. It was a relief, honestly, that Maria didn't have to get to know her.

She didn't even have to try.

"Here we are," Lyndsay mumbled. She was standing in front of a small car. In the dim light, it was hard to tell what color it was, but Maria thought it might be a silvery blue.

Lyndsay held the rear door open.

"You'll probably have to make room for yourself."

It took Maria just one glance inside to realize what she meant. The entire back seat was cluttered with what appeared to be empty takeout containers, fancy wrappers, and plastic bins.

This was a far cry from the arrivals she'd had at other temporary houses since her parents had died: plenty of taxis and cramped or overfilled family cars, yes, but always clean and hospitable ones.

Apparently Lyndsay wasn't going to try either.

Fine. Maria could deal with that.

She gritted her teeth as she crawled in, kicking away a cheery-looking plastic drink container.

"Sorry about that," Lyndsay said, finally sounding abashed. "I work in food—food writing. I was doing reviews for a friend who was on maternity leave, and I guess I . . . haven't really cleaned out the car."

Lyndsay yanked out a few of the bags, crumpling them in her hands and looking around for a trash bin.

Maria dragged in her suitcase and, after a moment's thought, balanced it over her lap.

The last thing it needed was another stain to make her look even more forgotten and left behind than she already was.

As she looked around in disgust, though, she realized something: not one of the containers was from a fast-food joint. At least, not one she recognized. They all looked ridiculously expensive.

"Okay," Lyndsay said with a sigh, rubbing her hands on her jeans as she walked back toward the car. "Now . . ."

There was the slight chime of a phone. It didn't even finish before Lyndsay had it to her ear. Maria stared at her face. Suddenly Lyndsay was all bright and pink cheeked.

Eager.

Excited.

Obviously this was the call she was waiting for.

"Hello?" she said breathlessly, getting into the driver's seat. "Yeah, hi, honey. I'm sorry, I saw you called earlier and I missed it. I was wondering how your presentation—"

She broke off. Maria watched as her shoulders sagged, and her face went from lit up to pale and anxious again.

Who was it? What had they said?

"Yes," Lyndsay mumbled. "Yes, she's here. We're in the car."

She glanced at Maria in the rearview mirror. Maria deliberately flicked a container that was leaning on her leg, making eye contact.

Yes, she was here, but not in a car. More like a trash can with wheels.

Lyndsay sighed and looked away.

"Did you want to talk to her . . . oh, no. I'm sorry. Yes, I understand. Yes, yes. I'll talk to you later, then—oh."

Lyndsay held the phone away, staring at the screen.

Maria's eyes widened before she could control them.

They hung up on her.

Talk about juicy. It was too interesting for even her to ignore.

"Who was that?"

Rather than answer, Lyndsay gave a tight smile.

"Okay, it's pushing five, and we have a bit of a drive ahead of us. Can you reach the seat belt?"

"No."

"Okay, then." Lyndsay strapped herself in. "I'll go slow."

Maria wondered if she could call Gillian and get herself sent back to Pakistan by explaining that her new guardian didn't believe in motor safety. Probably not. Adults covered for each other all the time.

As Lyndsay backed out, Maria stared at the window. There

was still no sign of light in the frosty gray sky. A knot grew in her stomach, in spite of herself.

She was used to being placed in the back of cars: different back seats, different city skylines to stare at as she approached them and then—after a few days of relatives converging, making decisions that were supposed to involve her but never did—left them behind.

But this felt different.

No one who knew her was in the car, making annoying small talk or turning on an old cassette of classic naats to fill the awkward silence, or sliding closer to the window in order to give her more space.

(Or, more likely, not catch the orphan bad luck hanging around her shoulders.)

No one was there to side-eye her as the car picked up speed, rushing forward past the payment meters. No one to try to figure out if she was as unperturbed as her sullen expression suggested. If she truly wasn't thinking about the other car they all had on their minds—the one her parents were riding in, in the distant faraway world of Australia, when they met their fate.

No one to whisper over her head in all-too-loud tones.

"I can't believe this child hasn't cried once. A heart of stone, she must have in that chest."

"They say she didn't even cry at the janazah. She stared into her parents' coffins and didn't say a word."

"Unpleasant."

Maria peeked at Lyndsay's face, its stark paleness reflected in the rearview mirror. She didn't seem to find anything unpleasant about Maria's stony silence. She didn't seem to worry at all about Maria's comfort, not even looking back.

That was a good thing.

She was, apparently, intent on not getting any more attached than Maria was. But it made Maria feel uneasy too . . . to be in the last place on Earth she wanted to be, driven into the heart of it by an utter stranger.

At least, until she realized, as Lyndsay pulled onto the highway, that they seemed to be headed in the opposite direction.

"Aren't we supposed to be going the other way?"

Lyndsay didn't bother to glance into the mirror.

"Manhattan? If you want to sightsee, we can do it one weekend while you're with us. But I'm sure you're going to get sleepy soon."

"Sightsee? You . . . don't live in New York City?"

Lyndsay's eyebrows raised.

"Oh. Well, no. Asra's the one who lives in the city. The Clayborne estate is out on Long Island. It'll be a long drive, because it's, like . . . right at the very end. You should get comfy."

The rest of her words flew over Maria's head.

She was still stuck on that phrase.

Long Island.

Not the city she'd been dreading stepping foot in since her aunt first told her that she was being sent away?

Maria straightened a little in her seat, trying to picture an island in her head. She'd never been to one, as the few homes she'd bounced between while her parents traveled were mostly land-locked, except for her naanu's house in Dhaka, Bangladesh. Long Island didn't sound like a place her parents would have liked. That suited her just fine.

There would be no ghosts waiting: no people they knew, people who would look her up and down and realize she didn't have her mother's smile (or, really, a smile at all, because what use did she have for one lately?) or her father's jokes.

Even Mr. Clayborne was on a business trip.

That meant she didn't have to take in the shimmering lights and life they had so loved, or try to imagine how they would have been and what they would have done.

Lyndsay reached for the radio, fumbling through crackling stations and occasional static as chilling and lurching as a sudden blast from the AC. She settled on something classical, and Maria leaned her head back against the seat and watched as the sun's light crept into the sky like a runny egg: watery and pale, still more of a winter's sunrise than a proper spring morning.

It was pretty, if you were into sunrises.

Maria found them to be overrated.

Watching as the city gave way to Long Island was more interesting.

It wasn't a sudden transformation, but a slow one. Buildings melted into trees, lots of them. They stood together, shoulder to shoulder, like masjid-goers in prayer, stretched by the side of the highway even as Lyndsay took turns and exits and shifted lanes. And amazingly enough, they were all still green.

"Evergreens," she said, catching Maria's fascinated stare out the window. "They don't die in the fall, so they stay green year-round. The others will be catching up soon enough."

Maria filed that word away. *Evergreen.*

It sounded like a hopeful word to have.

They must have traveled for an hour or more. Maria's eyes drooped, even though she tried to keep them open and take everything in through the window. She wanted to know where she was going, even if she didn't have a car to find her way back to the airport.

But in the end, she didn't even see which exit Lyndsay took.

She woke to a jostle and a muttered complaint from Lyndsay: "*Oh, come on.* I hate this road."

Maria sat upright, blinking and trying to take in her surroundings. Trees still lined both sides of the road, but it was no longer the wide belt of the highway.

Instead it was a little strip of residential road. She could see houses dotted in between the trees now, and as Lyndsay turned, the faint glint of water—a stream, maybe, or a small lake?—surrounded by a guardrail before it vanished behind more trees and more houses.

"We're almost there." Lyndsay grunted. "The road here is old, and narrow. So I have to be pretty careful . . . oh!"

Another car shot past, and Lyndsay lowered her own speed to a crawl. Maria gripped her armrest. Was this really safe?

But Lyndsay made it down the road, and the next turn resulted in a wider area.

"Just another turn to go," Lyndsay promised.

At the next turn, the houses got bigger, and more spaced apart: large mansions sprawling over green lawns, carefully guarded by tall fences with iron gates.

Occasionally Maria could see a glimpse of a covered pool.

Once or twice she saw a horse lift its head from grazing and stare toward the passing car.

"What is this place?" Maria breathed to herself. She'd seen rich-people houses before—a distant cousin in Hyderabad, India, had married a famous movie producer, and she remembered visiting for the wedding—but this was different.

This neighborhood was less colorful and lavish than those houses, and what the finer things in life looked like for Desi families in general. Here, there were benign tans and whites and browns. Back home, houses might be as bright orange as a syrupy jalebi on a platter, or the crisp red of a ten-taka Bangladeshi bill pressed into a palm for Eidi, holiday money from older relatives.

This was distant and desolate.

This was cold.

This was lonely.

Unease unfurled its petals in Maria's stomach.

Was this normal?

Phuppo's sniffles at the airport so many hours ago rang in the back of her mind. *"Don't be afraid, Maria. It will be different from what you know, but a good different."*

Maria had bristled at the very thought. Her? Afraid?

What was there to be afraid of?

Where other girls had shied away from going to the toilet

outdoors after dark, for fear of seeing a jinn, she had always hitched up her skirt and stomped her way in.

(Yes, she had always squeezed her eyes shut and kept her fists balled on her knees, just in case she needed to swing them. Yes, she had always rushed back out very quickly, without daring to look over her shoulder in case something—someone—was hovering there. But she had gone by herself, and that was what mattered.)

And of course she could walk past police officers and strange men as though they weren't there.

(But that didn't mean she didn't glance at their guns out of the corner of her eye. That didn't mean she wasn't aware of what clenched hands and cruel faces could do to a girl.)

Being afraid was a luxury other girls kept tucked in their drawers, along with perfume from their mothers and prized necklaces from their fathers.

Being afraid was what they could unfold and shake out, as beautiful and delicate as a shawl to hang around their shoulders, for the mere occasion of a bug crawling across their hand or a sudden clap of thunder.

Being afraid, for them, meant having their parents close enough to reassure them and wipe away their tears.

Who was Maria, to be afraid like that? Who did she have?

It took her a moment to realize that the radio was off.

She peeked at Lyndsay. The woman was sliding a piece of gum into her mouth, brow furrowed. The nails of the hand that still clutched the steering wheel were digging into the leather.

She didn't look happy to be getting closer to their destination.

She looked . . . resigned.

And then, after another moment . . .

"There it is." Lyndsay exhaled, and Maria's breath left her in one rolling rush too.

Yes, there it was.

The house.

IV ❧ *The House*

In Bangladesh

houses never show you what they are

at first glance.

Streets in Dhaka are lined with iron gates
barred windows
dusty sidewalk
faint flutter of curtains in upstairs windows
old tricycles and cluttered chairs on balconies.

Like the closed bud of a flower
you need to wiggle in and through
as a bee chases the faint smell of nectar
to see all that they truly are.

Overflowing courtyards
color speckled and life bold as the saris fluttering
over a seller's sleeve.
Neatly stitched rugs over tiled floors.
Zingy pop music unspooling from polished stereos.

Every room a little chamber of artfully presented delight
like jewel-toned sweets painstakingly arranged on delicate
pastel plates.

But maybe things are different here
in America
in New York.
        (Awful
        wrong
        shouldn't be here ever
                now
                without them
        New York.)

Because this house
the Clayborne house

tells Maria what it is right away
in every sagging, brown-black shingle
in the dark spikes dotting the top of the iron fence
in the wide porch that is wet in dripping shadow
in the dark bruise blue of the distant sea.

Unhappy.

This house is so very
unhappy.

Maria draws her dupatta closer around her throat
fighting back the chill not from the air but
from those hollow eyes that are the house's windows
from the porch that shrinks back from the morning sun's rays
from how very, truly, utterly
unhappy
this house is.

And how she, already so unhappy
so prickly
so bruised

will have to step inside
and see what dark, unpleasant secrets
hide behind its latched door.

Four

Most children have been told a lot about making an entrance.

Specifically, how not to make one.

Parents don't want children making too much of an entrance when they go to certain places, like the movie theater or a fancy restaurant.

And then, after lecturing a child about the importance of not making an entrance, they get upset when there isn't more of one at other times—like a graduation ceremony, or a party where they plan to show the child off to relatives.

Adults are contrary that way.

Maria always made as little of an entrance as possible, for the following reasons.

1. It didn't matter what she did or didn't do. She and

whichever unfortunate relative she was with were stuck together until they passed her on like a hot potato.

2. As it turned out, most adults didn't care even if you did try to make an entrance.

The second home Maria was sent to after her naanu's memory started getting bad was the only time she'd made an entrance. She arrived with a spit-polished face and a carefully worded introduction that she was not allowed to veer from in any way.

And she had done it.

She had stood there, as the adults sat around a low table studded with food for her arrival—not that she managed to taste much of it since she "needed to have manners."

With her hands folded and her face lowered, she recited her appreciation for their home and her hope that she wouldn't be a bother.

She looked up to see dull eyes and blank faces.

One of the aunties was lowering her hand from a yawn.

Oh, she got her cheek pinched, which she hated, and told that she was a good child (the only time she usually heard it) and how sorry everyone was for the circumstances she was visiting them under (emphasis on *visiting*), which she hated more.

But they were bored to tears.

So, as Maria followed Lyndsay up the steps and onto the porch, she wasn't mentally working through introductions or preparing to shake hands. She had her grasp steady on her bag: the best excuse not to have anyone reach for her or be expected to reach back.

"Oof," Lyndsay said through her teeth. "The key is stuck again."

She jiggled it in the lock, hissing with frustration. Maria shuffled away—not necessarily to give her space or anything Goody Two-shoes like that. Just to keep from getting an elbow to the face.

Maria's foot caught on the welcome mat. And as the key finally gave way under Lyndsay's grasp, Maria staggered forward through the open door.

Tumbling into the Clayborne house was the biggest entrance Maria had made in some time.

That was her only thought, as Lyndsay gasped behind her and she careened to a stop against a pair of legs.

"Goodness," a voice said above her.

Maria opened one eye, and then the other.

She was resting against a very elegant pair of trousers, neat pleats down each leg.

Maria looked up.

It was a woman, older, likely close in age to Phuppo's

mother, who had always sat in the corner of the living room to watch her dubbed Indian dramas and glowered whenever Maria so much as breathed a little too loudly.

Phuppo's mother had once said, without caring that Maria could hear, that Maria's mother was always a little too WILD and FLIGHTY.

A good woman would have been at HOME with her child once she was born, instead of GALLIVANTING around the world with her EQUALLY FOOLHARDY husband and not expecting SOMETHING BAD TO HAPPEN at SOME POINT.

(Never mind that the accident had happened on an ordinary residential road in an ordinary rental car, not in the middle of a war zone or any of the places her parents had volunteered in before.)

The woman standing above Maria now had that same sour pucker to her lips and the same distrust in her eyes.

She had short gray hair, with straight bangs that fell over her eyebrows, and lipstick in that same dark red that aunties seemed to reach for whether they were Kashmiri, or Punjabi, or apparently even white American.

"Do you need help?" she asked.

She didn't extend a hand.

"I'm fine," Maria mumbled, getting to her feet.

"Maria!" Lyndsay said behind her. For the first time,

her voice held some concern. "Oh, goodness. I should have warned you the floor is slick."

Maria kept an eye on the woman standing in front of her, arms folded.

It was then that Lyndsay seemed to notice her too.

"Oh! Charlotte," Lyndsay said. "I'm so sorry, I . . . did we wake you?"

The same energy from the phone call in the car was back. She sounded attentive.

No. Not just that—desperate to please.

Was this the person on the other side of the call? But no, then Lyndsay would've known that she was awake.

"I've been up since five," Charlotte said. Her gaze didn't leave Maria's face. "Is this her?"

"Yes, yes . . ." Lyndsay's hand fell on Maria, and she looked up into Lyndsay's face. Just like her voice, her entire expression seemed anxious.

"Maria, this is Charlotte. My . . . Mr. Clayborne's mother."

Maria had the very strong feeling that if she spoke first, she would automatically be deemed rude—but also that being silent was rude.

Simply, Charlotte was going to dislike her either way.

A minute passed. Charlotte cleared her throat.

"Well," she said. "It's nice to see you made it here. I'm sorry,

I find it so hard to manage before I get my morning coffee—"

"Coffee!" Lyndsay blurted out, letting her purse slip off her shoulder. "Oh, Charlotte, I'm so sorry. And breakfast—I really should have, before I went . . ."

Charlotte waved an elegant hand. "No, no, Lyndsay. Don't worry at all. Of course, when it is something for Ethan, I absolutely understand. It makes me happy to see that you can . . . be supportive."

The words themselves were mystifying, but there was no mistaking the biting undertone—or the way that Lyndsay's body jerked and her eyes widened, like an arrow had lodged beneath her skin.

It was only a moment.

And then, smiling, Charlotte turned on her heel and glided into the recesses of the house.

"One egg, please, Lyndsay."

Maria narrowed her eyes and made a mental note to keep as far away from Charlotte as possible.

"Of course," Lyndsay murmured. When Maria met her eyes, they were back to blank stillness.

"Well then," she said. "Let's have breakfast."

There was a minor upset, as Maria insisted on keeping her suitcase with her. She didn't trust these people yet, after all, and it felt wiser to have all her things nearby—just in case.

That wasn't being afraid. It was being careful.

Breakfast, which was served in a room that Lyndsay called the breakfast nook but just looked like a smaller dining room, was some weird-looking omelet and toast. Maria pushed it around her plate and tried to make it look like it was touched. It wasn't about sparing Lyndsay's feelings—it was making sure that neither of the adults reported to the alumni organization that she didn't want to eat or something.

Maria started when Charlotte cleared her throat, putting down her fork.

"Maria," she said. "That is your name, right?"

Of course she pronounced it wrong. Even so, Maria decided it was easier to answer. "Yes."

"I'm very sorry to hear about your parents. I know they were close to my son, so I am glad that he was able to have you . . . visit with us for a while. It would have been nice if my grandson, Colin, was here, so you would be occupied with someone your own age. But he's studying at an elite music conservatory, and it's the middle of his semester."

Charlotte's words were polite, but again, Maria could hear that this lady wasn't happy having her here. That wasn't surprising.

But that she seemed determined to have a conversation, rather than making her unhappiness clear, was odd.

"I hope you know that we're here to help you feel as comfortable as possible," Charlotte continued. "All right?"

"Okay."

Charlotte laid down her fork, her brow furrowing.

Apparently one-word answers weren't what she wanted.

"Well. It seems you're shy, so I'll give you time to warm up. But in the meantime, I think it would be best if we laid out some rules."

"Charlotte," Lyndsay broke in, her voice strained. "Ethan said he wanted her to feel at home. . . ."

Charlotte raised her hand. "Please don't interrupt, Lyndsay. I know what Ethan has said, but this is a historic estate full of valuable family history. Lines need to be drawn now, just the same as we would for Colin if he was home."

Lyndsay pursed her lips but fell silent.

"It would be best to keep to the first floor and your room," Charlotte said, turning her firm gaze back on Maria. "My suite is strictly off-limits, as are the rooms on the third floor. This is for your own good as well. The house is big, and old, and it's easy to get lost. You understand me, right?"

Maria did.

Loud and clear.

The message was, *You don't belong here, no matter what my son says. You need to remember your place.*

She would.

She didn't even want to be here, much less bother with their stuffy "family history" and disgusting omelets. But she was sure saying so would scandalize Lyndsay and earn a further lecture from Charlotte. So she pushed her food to one side of her plate and stood.

"I'd like to see my room now so I can unpack and pray. If that's okay."

If they wanted to set rules, she'd play along.

"Yes, Maria," Lyndsay said, standing up hastily. "Of course." Her plate looked just as untouched as Maria's.

"One more thing," Charlotte added. "You should also limit your time outside. I do have some plants out there that don't take well to roughhousing or running about with sneakers on."

Maria's ears perked up.

Plants? She did like plants.

Lyndsay interjected. "She's a kid. She's going to want to explore. Wouldn't it be better if she does that outside?"

Her voice was even, but Maria didn't miss the look she shot Maria out of the corner of her eye. Lyndsay was obviously thinking about the horrors of Maria having to be inside all the time, and being responsible for the girl's entertainment.

Charlotte's lips compressed.

"We will see," was all she said.

Maria reached for her suitcase without a word.

Yes, she would play by the rules.

At least until she was out of their sight.

Because, out of everything in this cold, unhappy house, a garden sounded most promising.

Five

The second floor was disappointingly normal.

From the outside of the house and the large, cold living room, Maria was expecting something more . . . dark and broody. But the stairwell was bright, cheery yellow, leading into a hallway lined with soft carpet and with half-open doors spilling out sunlight.

"My room, if you need anything at night," Lyndsay said, waving a hand down toward the farthest end of the hallway. "The bathroom. Storage closet. Charlotte's room is over there."

Maria caught a glimpse of a large bed and pristine white walls. Charlotte didn't have to worry about Maria going into her room. It looked far too boring.

"And here's your room," Lyndsay announced, pushing the door nearest the stairs open with her foot. The room was small, with pale pink walls and a bed shoved up underneath the window. It looked exactly like the room Lyndsay and Charlotte would think a girl would want.

"I hope you like it," Lyndsay said with a frown. "It's a little empty. Mr. Clayborne wanted us to do more decorating, but it was such short notice . . ."

"I don't mind that," Maria mumbled, kicking off her shoes and wrinkling her nose at the sight of frilled pillows piled on the bed.

The room did seem unfinished. The angled dresser looked dragged in, and there was a pile of boxes in the corner bearing labels—BEDROOM DECOR, STORAGE BINS, SPARE CURTAINS.

It wasn't anything like the rooms before, in Bangladesh or Pakistan or even Belgium, rooms she always shared in some way, whether it was lying her head in her naanu's lap and dozing off to rhythmic pats on her back as her grandmother and aunts chattered over her head, or her parents curled up on her floor with their laptops and notebooks to keep her company while she did her own homework.

And that was fine. That life was gone.

"You don't? I mean . . . well . . ." Lyndsay shook her head.

"I guess that's good then. If you need an extra hand hanging up your clothes—"

"I'm good."

Lyndsay hugged her arms around herself and stared around the room again.

"I do want you to be comfortable here," she said finally. "Okay? Don't worry about bothering me, all right? I'm usually in the kitchen."

She had that desperate smile back on, the one from earlier. So Maria just nodded.

"Okay."

Finally she left. Maria sat on the bed, disgustedly pushing some of the frilly pillows aside to make space. Her nose itched from dust, and her stomach hurt from the gross omelet.

But most of all, her heart ached, and she wasn't even sure why.

Enough of that.

Maria rose to her feet. Charlotte Clayborne might have told her to stay away from the third floor, but she was Maria Latif.

And no one kept Maria Latif from exploring.

She tentatively peered into the hallway. Lyndsay had already shuffled back downstairs. From the crisp sound of

BBC News drifting up the stairs, Charlotte was still down there too.

Good.

Maria tiptoed toward the half-open doors, peeking into each. Nothing seemed any more interesting than the glimpses she had gotten earlier.

Maybe the next floor would be. The upper staircase did look less taken care of, compared to the carpeted stairs leading to this floor—splintered and dusty, and very, very old.

But Maria could handle dust. She raised her foot—

And was nearly bowled over by a sudden gust of wind, cold and biting as though she'd stuck her head into a freezer. She clung to the railing for balance, gasping for air.

What was that?

She stared up the staircase, trying to see an open door, or maybe a window. But all above her was dark and still.

Warm air billowed around her sock feet. After that angry blast, it felt soothing—almost like fingers curled around her ankle, coaxing her back down the stairs toward comfort and safety.

It was a good thing Maria didn't mind the cold. She gritted her teeth and stepped forward again.

The stair under her foot gave a high-pitched screech, and she leaped back.

A chill ran down her spine.

What was going on?

But then she pulled herself together. Ridiculous to think it was anything more than a typical old house.

Stop it, she told herself, and shook her head firmly before taking the steps two at a time.

Each stair creaked loudly, and on the last one she paused, sure there had been a change in the loud noise of the BBC— that Charlotte had risen off the couch to check on her, that Lyndsay had emerged from the kitchen to call her name. But there was nothing.

And to Maria's disappointment, the third floor was just as boring as the second.

Usually adults go through all the trouble of making rules to hide something interesting, but the third floor was simply less decorated.

Until Maria looked more closely.

There were spots on the wall where pictures used to hang, probably eons ago. The carpet was faded, and the doors Maria pushed open led to storage cabinets and old rooms with drop cloths tossed over furniture.

As she passed one door, though, she heard something impossible: a low, soft lilt, familiar as birdsong. She froze. Goose bumps raised on her arms.

"It can't be," she whispered, half to herself and half to the house.

The rabab, Kashmir's king of music—the instrument's voice aching and full of longing to be home. The sound of it brought tears to her eyes.

It couldn't be. But it was.

Nothing else sounded so sweet and yet so sad. Nothing else spoke in the voice of the refugee as much as the refugee's instrument itself. That's what her father always said.

"The first time I heard a rabab," he had said, "I understood what it was saying to me. Because I too had to leave my home. I too had to leave without knowing if I would ever come back."

She was little then, her hair in the short bob that her mother said all Bangladeshi children wore at some point in their lives.

"It's a rite of passage," she said, pushing back the bangs to kiss Maria's furrowed brow. "You look so cute. Such a sweet baby."

Maria was sure she looked like a mushroom. A grumpy one.

Like her mother, her father was always pushing back her fringe. He did it at that moment, with a soft, sad little laugh.

"I thought Pakistan was your home," Maria said curiously.

"It is, and it isn't. Kashmir is my home. But there's no

going back to it. The rabab knows that, and it sings to comfort us, the people who can never go back."

Thinking of her father brought a funny feeling to Maria's throat, like there was a lump there she couldn't swallow. She forced the thoughts of him away.

How could a rabab possibly be here?

It was not a common instrument for the United States—at least, outside of gatherings of people who'd left their homelands with the dogs of war chasing after them, trying to sink teeth into their heels.

There was only silence now. When she tried the doorknob, it didn't turn. She stared at it for a moment. She hated how this house was making her feel already.

But she had to keep moving.

Finally the last door at the end of the hall gave her something she didn't expect: a set of stairs, likely to an attic. Maria stared at it.

Charlotte hadn't said anything about an attic. Had she forgotten about it?

These steps were even more rickety than the others, and Maria worked hard to keep her footing. She stumbled on the last one, coming face-to-face with a fat, juicy spider in a web. She shuddered and pulled back. Maria Latif was many things, but spiders were definitely where she drew the line at rushing in.

As she paused, she stared down at her foot. When she'd jumped back, there hadn't been a creak or a moan, or a little sigh from the wooden step. Why were these stairs so quiet when they were in worse shape than the others?

The attic was cluttered with old furniture. Maria picked her way through, moving drop cloths that clung like moss aside to examine what was underneath and lifting curtains. Unlike the unused rooms downstairs, this furniture was ornate. There were elegant couches, carved chests heaped with china, and in one, a glimmer of silk that Maria lifted out carefully.

She gasped. It was a sari—a wedding sari, heavily embroidered and bright red.

Who would wear a wedding sari in this house?

She stroked it, chilled by how cold it was.

She moved toward the half-raised window, looking out into the vastness of the yard behind the house. Charlotte seemed most reluctant about her stepping foot outside, which was weird.

Every other relative who'd taken Maria in had quickly realized that tossing her outdoors was the best way to deal with her. She might be sitting in a corner and poking a stick into the dirt and talking to herself, but at least she wasn't, say, causing family discord by blurting out a rumor she should not have known directly to a respected elder's face.

Everyone learned to pick their battles with Maria.

Toward the back of the yard, an ornate greenhouse caught her eye. The glass walls glimmered like a diamond in the morning light.

Maybe that was why Charlotte was so antsy about her going out there.

She was about to turn away when something flickered across the glass.

Maria leaned in.

A little lizard stared back at her from the windowpane.

"Ah!" Maria jumped, and her elbow collided with the little creature. The lizard tumbled from view.

Maria stared after it. It had looked like a tik-tiki, a common house gecko—but what would it be doing somewhere so cold?

Had it just been her imagination?

She jerked the window down and hoped that no one had heard her little outburst.

And then something else glimmered in the distance. Far into the recesses of the property, down the winding path leading from the neatly groomed lawn and greenhouse and accompanying shed and empty flower beds . . .

Green.

Lots of green.

What was that?

Maria craned her head but could not see more.

"And what are you doing up here?"

Maria's head collided with the glass. "Ouch!"

She turned to see Charlotte, arms folded and face stern.

Uh-oh.

"Exploring."

"I thought I told you earlier that these floors were off-limits."

"Not this one."

Charlotte's eyes widened. She wasn't expecting that.

"Excuse me?"

"You said the third floor," Maria said primly. "This is the attic."

"Well, you can only get here from the third floor. You were asked to stay close to your room."

Charlotte strode forward.

"This attic is full of valuables, and I won't have you playing in here." Her eyes narrowed as she took in Maria's position by the window. What were you looking at out there?"

"Oh, uh . . ." Maria looked back at the window. The lizard was gone. The green glimmer was gone. "The yard, I guess."

Charlotte pursed her lips. "Remember the rules, Maria. Don't wander off through the yard without checking in with Lyndsay or me first. Understand?"

"Yes," Maria said. But she didn't look at Charlotte. Her eyes were still on the window.

Because wandering through the yard seemed like an excellent idea.

Six

Charlotte Clayborne wasn't the boss of Maria Latif.

Maria wasn't sure what was going on with the tik-tiki, and the glimpse of green, and the gusty, creepy—except when it wasn't—house, but she was determined to figure it all out.

She did unpack, just a little. She took one of her plain dupattas and spread it on the floor and prayed, though she guiltily kept an ear craned downward, waiting. She hoped God could forgive her distraction, just this once.

Eventually the TV sounds resumed, and she picked her way back down the stairs with her shoes in hand. Charlotte seemed to be in the breakfast nook, from the sounds of a coffee cup clinking against the table and occasional clucks of disapproval toward the news.

There was no sign of Lindsay, so Maria skirted the kitchen and made her way toward the back of the house. She passed closed doors but wasn't tempted to poke her head in. Charlotte and Lindsay didn't seem concerned about keeping her away from anything on this floor.

Finally she reached an old wooden door lined on either side by scuffed rain boots and rusted tools. Maria glanced over her shoulder as she slipped on her shoes, but it didn't seem like anyone had followed her. She walked out, and into the backyard.

As she tromped around the yard, she poked into a few bushes by the wall of the house. There was no sign of the lizard. Had she imagined it?

"Are you looking for something?" The unfamiliar voice came from behind Maria.

She nearly jumped out of her skin, whirling around.

"Wha—"

A girl stood at the entrance to the backyard, smiling at her. Or rather, dimpling. Her sweet brown face seemed to be made up of two aggressive dimples, framed on either side by long French braids.

Dimple girl was definitely older than Maria was, with little golden hoop earrings and a T-shirt that shouted TIME TO ROCK AND ROLL!

Maria was instantly wary.

"Who are you?" she asked.

"Around here, we start with salaam, or hi, or both," the girl countered. Her smile didn't get any smaller, though, and she didn't move. "But that's okay. I freaked you out. Sorry about sneaking up on you like that."

"I wasn't freaked out."

"Oh, of course. Sorry." The girl moved forward, extending a hand. "I'm Mahajabeen Rehman. But you can call me Mimi. This year, at least. I may be someone else next year. I live two streets down. I heard a kid moved in, and that's not really usual for this neighborhood, so I wanted to investigate."

Maria looked at the hand. Oh. So she was a Cool Girl.

It was hard to explain Cool Girls to adults, because they got all disappointed and said things like, "It sounds like she wants to be your friend" or "Why are you talking about her like that, like she's a mean girl?"

But Cool Girls weren't mean at all. That was the problem.

They were always dependable, good at keeping friends, and remembered to send thank-you cards without their parents asking. They had good grades, and better dreams for the future.

And they never, ever scowled.

When Maria's mom was alive, she had been intent on

making Maria a Cool Girl. Which, of course, did not and would never happen.

Even her mom knew it.

"I wish Maria could be as sweet outside as she is here. She just gets so . . . prickly," Ammu would sigh to Baba when she thought Maria wasn't listening.

Maria wasn't sure why that still stung.

It didn't matter now, anyway. Being prickly, unpleasant Maria was her thing. It kept adults wary of her. That was what mattered.

But ever since overhearing her mom's remarks, Maria had been uneasy around Cool Girls.

Cool Girls always seemed to sense that she was supposed to be one of them in another life—one where her mom was home more often, and Maria had basked in Ammu's confident, airy starshine enough to carry on the way Cool Girls did.

They also seemed able to tell that, because she wasn't one of them after all, she would be told, "Oh, why can't you be more like that girl?"

And to make up for it, they became even nicer and more worried about her when they could.

More pitying.

Her cousins were Cool Girls, offering to lend her their

shalwar kameez for parties, trying to loop her into their friends' conversations.

This girl looked like that type. And Maria wasn't here for it.

"Nice to meet you," Maria muttered. "Bye."

But the girl ignored the hint for her to move along. She gazed around the yard.

"Wow, this place is massive!"

That caught Maria's attention. She looked at Mimi out of the corner of her eye.

"Yours isn't?"

"Well, I guess it's big. Most houses here are, because we're near the Hamptons. A lot of famous people live around here, so the houses have to be big and flashy too, right? But this is definitely bigger than usual."

Hamptons? Rich and famous?

Maria just nodded like she understood.

"I've only ever seen it from the street. It's a lot when you're right next to it." Mimi looked around, an awed look on her face, before something caught her attention.

"What's back there?"

Of course she was pointing deep into the back of the yard, where Charlotte didn't want her exploring. Where Maria had seen that tantalizing glimpse of green. Maria sighed and rolled her eyes.

"I don't know. It's private."

"Hmm." The girl peered toward it intently.

Maria was trying to figure out another, even less polite way to tell her that she should be going, but Mimi's next words made her freeze.

"That must be where the garden is."

"What?"

Mimi didn't look at her, nodding decisively.

"Yeah, you know, the one everyone used to talk about? My dadima says the neighbors used to call it the Hanging Gardens of Babylon. It looks like there's enough room back there."

"Hmm," Maria muttered absently, imitating the girl's earlier response. The wheels in her head were spinning.

A garden that the Claybornes were now choosing to hide away instead of show off? Why do that in a neighborhood where having a prominent garden was worth gossiping about?

Both girls startled as a call rang from the house.

"Maria! Are you out there?"

Lyndsay, giving a subtle hint not to wander too far—probably egged on by Charlotte. Maria sighed.

"Sounds like it's time for you to head in. Anyway, it was nice to meet you, Maria." Mimi dimpled again. "I'm sure we'll see more of each other."

I hope not, Maria thought dourly.

At least she had some new information to turn over in her head: a garden that no one wanted her near.

She had to get back out here soon.

V ❧ *The Photo Album*

When you've explored all the outer walls,

go inward.

That was always the rule,
    Maria found,
in hide-and-seek
and understanding adults
and searching a house

for a secret she didn't quite yet understand.

So, as gray skies churned outside her windows
and rain beat a lulling refrain against the roof
when her guardians' eyes were turned to TV screen and
mixing bowl,
    she turned her investigation
to floorboards and closet shelves
rather than closed bedroom doors and bathroom cabinets.

The bottom of the closet was where she found it:
the album.

Bound in old, smeared plastic,
pages shedding dust like scale-heavy butterfly wings.

She flipped through with care,
lingering over familiar-looking faces on strangers,
clothing in patterns that gave her pause,
sure that she might have clung to the waist of this
unknown woman
or brushed past this Bengali lungi-clad uncle
while pelting by in pursuit of some childhood mischief.

But nothing was
an inner wall
nothing was
an unbreached secret

at least
until the last page.
The page that had a young man—
tall, mopey, long-haired, with the weight of the world
on slouched shoulders
arm around another

whose face was not just familiar
but dear

a face she has kissed on the cheek before bed
a face who had laughed and called her
his darling little girl
a face she did not know when he was
so young, and will not see when he is so old.

Her father.

And Mr. Clayborne.

It must be.

She took a moment to breathe
to gather
from within her own hidden rooms
and inner secrets
a bit of calmness
and then turned the page.
And here was a picture that made her heart flutter.

Here was something that made her mind turn cartwheels
of surprise
    and wonder
    and consideration
    and determination.

Because here was the proof that she must go outside
and see what she could of this estate and its green lawn
    so cut off from the outside world.

Her parents
    both of them
    young
    beautiful
    shimmering, luminous stars
sitting in a garden
    blossoms shedding pink petals on their dark heads.

It could not be Pakistan
or Bangladesh.

Was it out there,
    in the yard?

She didn't know.

Yet.

Seven

At first it didn't seem like escaping outside again would be easy.

Lyndsay was the straightforward one of the adults to deal with. After a few rainy days stuck inside, Maria realized that Lyndsay's routine was fairly simple: wake up and cook breakfast (which, it turned out, could be good, as long as it was something she had decided to make and not Charlotte), then hide in the kitchen and mysteriously clatter pots and pans with the door closed for the rest of the day.

Charlotte was another matter. Though Maria had snuck outside successfully once, she was very much caught on the way in. Charlotte narrowed her eyes at her grass-stained pants and dirty hands.

"You won't be doing that again," she said sternly.

"I like it out there," Maria said stubbornly. "I like fresh air. It's too dusty in here."

"Not in the living room. Don't kids your age like TV?"

"I don't."

Charlotte sighed and shook her head.

"Find something else to do, Maria. I have ideas, if you want."

No, thank you. Maria moped about her room the first afternoon. The second, she found that she could slide around on the slick wood floor of the breakfast nook in her sock feet.

Charlotte apparently didn't like her doing that either.

By the third morning, Maria was downright bored.

And she hated being bored.

She slid the previous day's clothes over her head after a tentative sniff. She didn't feel like rummaging in her suitcase again to find something new. Tiptoeing out into the hallway, shoes in hand, she shuddered.

It was so much colder this morning than it had been last night. At night, it felt different in her room—warm enough that she'd almost been fooled she was back in Lahore. Or Dhaka. It almost smelled like it too—the henna scent of her naanu's hair and the ever-present tingle of peppery spices in the air. But that had to be her imagination. Now the house felt chilly and empty, and she hurried in spite of herself down the stairs and toward the hallway leading to the back door.

Charlotte's voice, though, made her stop in her tracks.

"Lyndsay, don't tell me you want the child to go outside."

"Well, there's more room for her out there, Charlotte," came Lyndsay's voice. It sounded like she was in the kitchen, while Charlotte was already seated in the breakfast nook. "Of course, I don't want to overstep. . . ."

"You wouldn't be overstepping, dear. You're a Clayborne, after all. I wish you would act like it."

"I . . . yes, of course, Charlotte."

Maria craned her head around the corner of the living room, watching as Charlotte frowned into the cup like the coffee was to blame for her perpetually sour mood.

"Well," Lyndsay's voice came again, soft and tentative, "it doesn't look like she did any harm when she slipped out the other day. And she even made a friend."

"Harm that we can see from the window." Charlotte snorted. "God only knows what could happen if she wanders too close to . . . oh my goodness!" She jumped, her cup clattering against the table as she caught sight of Maria. "Do you always walk like a ghost?"

"Yes," Maria replied. She was irritated with herself. Another moment, and Charlotte would have let something particularly juicy slip. "What were you talking about?"

Charlotte narrowed her eyes. "How you won't be breaking the rules by sneaking outside. Goodness, sit down."

"I'm not hungry. And I like it outside."

"You do need to eat, Maria," Lindsay broke in, appearing from the kitchen with two sunny yellow plates in hand. She slid one toward an empty seat, tilting her head toward Maria. "Eat, and maybe you can go outside."

"Eat, and maybe you can look through something for me," Charlotte countered with a stern look. She turned her gaze to Maria. "I have a bunch of pamphlets I've gathered for you. Day camps, library activities . . . opportunities for you to occupy yourself for the time being, while we work on enrolling you in school."

"No," Maria said sharply, and added "thank you" at the panicked look Lyndsay shot her. She sat down and stared at the plate. It was a good breakfast this morning—fresh pancakes, the aroma of syrup and rivulets of butter and a faint hint of pumpkin spice rising up—but she didn't feel hungry.

How was she going to get back outside?

Charlotte cleared her throat, patting her mouth delicately. "I'll be upstairs this morning. I've got a few birthday cards to send to the extended family. Lyndsay?"

Lyndsay jumped to her feet, quickly gathering the plates and darting toward the kitchen. The door slid closed behind her.

"Hiding again," Charlotte muttered. Or at least, that was how it sounded.

A moment later, she looked up, her eyes sharp on Maria's face.

"And just what are you doing?"

"Nothing," Maria said, grabbing her shoes. It seemed like it was best to beat a hasty retreat to her room. Again.

When she passed the closed kitchen door, though, she paused. The kitchen faced toward the yard. Could it have a door to the outside?

She walked in.

Lyndsay didn't even look up. She was frowning, glasses balanced on the bridge of her nose as she glanced quickly between a notepad on the counter and a bubbling pot.

"So how many minutes should this . . ."

Maria lifted on her tiptoes, curious in spite of herself. She peered down at the pot.

"Should it what?"

Lyndsay nearly jumped out of her skin.

"Maria! Could you . . . please make more noise!"

Maria ignored her. Adults were always so jumpy, and it

was only ever their fault for not listening more closely to their surroundings.

"What is that supposed to be?"

Lyndsay sighed again. She stepped away from the pot and inclined her head.

"Take a look."

Maria peered in at the mushy contents.

"What is that?"

"I was testing a recipe for paella, but now I'm not sure what it is."

"It looks like khichuri, honestly," Maria said. She wasn't sure why she was offering anything to Lyndsay, particularly when the woman wasn't even looking at her, but it was the first time she'd seen her at work.

Now Lyndsay looked at Maria with interest. Her face was open and curious.

"Khichuri?"

"It's like . . . soggy rice," Maria said, trying to find the right words. "Or maybe porridge?"

"Porridge? Like congee?" Lyndsay lifted the spoon experimentally to her mouth and then snapped her fingers. "Yep, my paella turned into a congee. Well, at least I can let the magazine know this recipe was a wash."

"What's wrong with congee?"

Maria sniffed it again. It didn't smell like much, but if congee was like khichuri—all savory and warm and perfect with a boiled egg on the side—there was potential.

"Nothing . . ." Lyndsay trailed off, thoughtfully, her eyes distant. "My grandma always made congee when I was sick. My Taiwanese grandma, I mean. This was a long time ago."

"So, do you know the recipe?" Maria asked.

Lyndsay's eyes sharpened, and all of a sudden, she looked like a different person: firmer, more determined.

"I think I can figure it out. Thank you."

Maria blinked. She hadn't meant to help at all, only . . .

"Now I need space to work," Lyndsay said firmly. "Fun's over. Time for you to find something else to do."

Maria rolled her eyes.

"You don't have to push me. I'm going."

Part of her definitely regretted helping Lyndsay. But she was more irritated with herself. How had she forgotten so quickly that she wasn't here to make friends with Lyndsay while the outside awaited? After all, there was indeed a door to the yard at the other end of the kitchen.

Now was her chance. She slipped her shoes on.

"I'm going out for air!"

The door swung closed before Lyndsay could respond.

Rice porridge still lingering on her tongue, Maria stood on the porch and stared out over the yard.

It was time to find that glint of green.

First, though, she needed to take a peek into Charlotte's sacred greenhouse. It didn't look like much on the outside, but considering how determined the woman was to keep her out, who knew?

Maria trod carefully, glancing over her shoulder once or twice. But the house stayed quiet and the door didn't bang open, so it seemed like she was safe. She peered in through the windows. They were sparkling and clear—not a sign of dust on the frames or the sills. Inside was a tiled walkway, hanging baskets with fern fronds spiraling out and neat rows of potted plants.

Bo-*ring*. And not worth being caught over. Maria slid back, making sure she left no smudges on the glass. There was something about Charlotte that made her sure the woman would be able to spot one from inside the house.

Maria Latif wasn't scared of anything, but she also wasn't a fool.

So that left the path beyond the greenhouse.

What was it that girl Mimi had said her dadima called the garden?

The Hanging Gardens of Babylon.

Maria remembered them now. They were one of the old Seven Wonders of the World in ancient times, and the king who built them for his wife didn't do so for fun. It was because he'd taken her far away from her home, and he wanted her happy and not homesick.

Maria shook her head disgustedly. Grown-ups—and Mimi also, apparently—found the worst things utterly romantic.

As she walked farther back, empty but neatly prepared flower beds gave way to a meandering path, closed in by large trees and guided by a barely visible stone walkway.

She didn't realize it was leading her somewhere until she was standing in front of it.

Maria's breath left her in a gasp.

"Oh, *wow.*"

An iron fence loomed before her. She couldn't see through the bars, as there were wooden planks lining the other side, but she still rushed up and tried to peer in.

Through the slightest gap, she saw a flash of green that made her heart pound.

Yes. This *had* to be it.

She drifted along the fence, hand trailing the bars, until it met with what had to be the gate. It was curlicued and fancy, and . . .

Maria groaned.

There was a padlock, right where the gate met the fence.

"Now what?"

She stood back, hands on her hips.

There was no way she could ask Lyndsay about a key without clueing her—or Charlotte, or worse both—in to the fact that she was trying to get in somewhere she shouldn't.

But she was so close.

She bit her lip in frustration. She couldn't really explain, even to herself, why Mimi's story of an abandoned garden had gotten under her skin, or why the sight of that green out the window had made her heart pound faster.

Perhaps it was because the house felt so constricting, so enveloping and utterly surrounding in its sad silence.

Or maybe it was because she hated being told what to do.

She was about to double back, toward the shed near the greenhouse, which had to have some tools in it, maybe even the key—when a flash of green dashed forward. It nearly collided with her fingers, still wrapped around the iron bars of the gate.

"Ah!"

Maria stumbled backward, eyes wide.

A little lizard was wrapped around the bars, blinking its large eyes at her.

"The tik-tiki," she breathed. She hadn't imagined it.

She wasn't fond of tik-tikis. There was something off-putting about turning your head in the middle of the night in Bangladesh, and seeing a lizard staring back. But they didn't freak her out the way they did her cousins.

"What do you want?" she demanded. "And how are you here? Did you get lost?"

The tik-tiki didn't answer. Of course she didn't expect it to. But then it wiggled its little body toward the padlock.

The padlock shifted. Just a bit. Maria gasped.

"It's not locked! Did you—no, of course not."

Maria reached out and worked with her nail. The tik-tiki moved back.

Any other day, Maria would have been bothered by the fact that she thought that a *lizard* was helping her, but right now she was too excited to care.

The padlock fell to the ground with a heavy thud. For a moment, all Maria could hear was her own harsh breath, and the pounding of her heart. The tik-tiki wasn't there anymore. It probably felt its mission was done. Unease shivered up her spine, but she shook it off.

The gate was waiting.

She pushed it open. It gave, slowly, painfully, with a long, rasping creak. When it was just wide enough, she slipped through.

Into the garden.

VI ✍ *The Garden*

Maria was used to gardens that greeted you like family:
drippingly dramatic,
doused in perfume and lush colors,
leaves flung open like waiting arms,
wide and inescapable,
brushing against your sleeves,
giving you their attention
even when you thought you
had done your best to avoid it
by withholding yours.

In Lahore, she snuck through her aunt's courtyard,
coaxing those giddy buds off their stems,
popping them into her pockets
where through the layers of cotton,
she could hear them
offering her tea
urging her to sit
suffusing her with the sensations of a world
that seemed too bright and beautiful to be true.

And
of course
it always was.

The buds drew in upon themselves
winking shut like shocked mouths
keeping their own counsel
as Maria tried to use finger and nail to unfurl
the pretty greetings and blushing charm
she was once offered.

They grew tired of kindnesses
lavished on a stony face
and mournful orphan-child whites.
Their blossoms didn't seem to leave even
a smear of pigment.

Gardens preferred
when you were a guest.

Gardens preferred
when you were gilded like them
or else did not linger
and remind them that the world outside
also came in shades of gray.

But not this garden.

How does this garden grow, Maria?
Not at all.
Nothing but empty pots
mossy trunks
and earth.

Maria knelt.
She put her fingers in the ground
and listened.
The soil did not offer her tea.
It did not ask her to speak louder
sit closer
tell it all about where she'd been.
It did not try to coax blooming cheeks
onto her face
or find a color that wasn't worn and weary

in her clothes.

But.
It hummed.
It thrummed.

And Maria smiled.

This
(unloved
untouched
unclaimed)
bit of earth
would be hers.

Eight

Maria wasn't sure what she expected to find behind that creaking iron gate.

Not the lush, flower-laden tree boughs and vines creeping up over the iron handles of the bench from the picture of her parents.

And she was not silly enough to imagine her parents would be waiting with their arms outstretched to draw her into their laps and try to pinch a smile onto her scowling face.

How can you look like that, ma, when we're here with you in such a beautiful place?

She tried not to let it bother her—how, in that picture, her parents were smiling widely, basking in sunlight without any files spread over their laps or papers held to rehearse speeches.

Looking peaceful. Content.

Just fine.

Without her there.

Maria drew in a breath and shook her head. It didn't matter now. Could that bench under that withered tree be the one from the picture? If she *had* found the garden, then it needed her.

Where was the green she'd seen out the attic window? Most of the main plot was clogged with decaying leaves from what looked like last autumn. Maria could just make out little signs prodding their way through the rot, but what was on them—if there was anything left on them—she couldn't tell. Whatever plants they were meant to identify were long gone, anyway.

There were a lot of weeds to clear away, particularly along the formerly neat stone path.

Still, it wasn't a complete disappointment. It would need work, but Maria could work.

Maria stood underneath the large overhanging tree and stared down at the iron bench. It looked too splintered to safely take a seat on, and the tree was withered, its bare branches sweeping the ground as though in defeat.

Hanging off one forlorn, rusted armrest was a piece of cloth. Maria reached out but couldn't bring herself to touch it.

It was so mildewed and tattered, its color so washed out she couldn't even tell what it was. A forgotten coat? A silk shawl?

As though responding to the nearness of her hand, the fabric billowed upward in a sudden breeze. It nuzzled against her fingertips, and she recoiled at the sensation of slimy cloth.

"Ew!" She shook out her hand, scowling down at it—and then took a closer look.

"No way. Is that . . ."

She could see it now, the just-there remnants of once-resplendent embroidery that trailed along its sides.

It was a sari. At least, the very edge of one, still sticking out and begging to be tugged by a child's hand the way it would have been when worn.

Maria backed away. Why would a sari be left out here in a garden long gone to seed?

Because someone died, a little voice hissed in her head. *It's a memorial.*

Or a tomb, like the Taj Mahal.

Only moments ago, the entire garden had been drenched in welcoming sunlight, but now shadows drew in around her. The distant sounds from farther down the street turned ghostly.

"Ugh," Maria muttered, rubbing her arms.

That was nonsense. Babies believed in ghosts, but Maria knew they didn't exist. Old aunties constantly clucked about jinn possessing people and tampering in human affairs, but that didn't mean Maria expected one of them to bother her. In Phuppo's favorite TV shows, jinn were always preoccupied with pretty, fainting heroines anyway.

Maria glanced at the bench again, and choked on a scream.

Something bulged beneath the sari's fabric, a little, moving *lump*.

Maria's mind went wild. *A hand! A jinn coming back for its forgotten clothes!* She stumbled back.

"I'm not scared of you," she gasped. "Just . . . take what you want and leave me alone."

One heel caught on her other boot, and she toppled to the ground, barely catching herself with her hands. They scraped against the cold, hard-packed earth, but she could hardly feel it.

All her attention was on the moving lump, making its way closer and closer to the edge of the fabric. Maria held her breath, and it felt as though the whole garden—every withered tree and pile of dead leaves—leaned in to watch.

And then, out from under the fabric, popped a little green head.

Not human, but not jinn, either. A little lizard head.

The tik-tiki blinked up at Maria, seemingly unaware that he'd just scared several years off her life.

"You again," Maria snapped, pushing herself up and dusting off her bottom and trying not to feel silly.

The tik-tiki cocked its head and scuttled toward the edge of the bench, leaping into a little thatch of weeds.

Maria exhaled and looked around the garden once more. It wasn't a ghostly haunt, or a beautiful hideaway.

But it was Maria's.

She needed tools, some way to gather up the dead leaves and examine the soil. And after that, she would need new plants.

Excitement bubbled in her chest. Even the thought of figuring out a way to get all she needed couldn't daunt her.

She was going to make this garden as green as she had imagined it to be.

Nine

The next morning, Maria awoke in her parents' house.

She had curled up the night before in the small, dusty bed in her small, dusty room on Long Island, listening to the sounds of Lyndsay brushing her teeth and Charlotte grumbling to herself as old women always did as she made her way to her own room down the hall.

But when Maria startled awake, her mouth was dry and skin sweaty.

Her shalwar kameez sleeves stuck like wet paper to her arms. The entire room felt like a gently simmering oven.

And the sound—

It was a low hum that, at first, sounded like music. But soon it became distant voices.

Familiar voices.

Her heart pounded, and tears prickled the corners of her eyes.

She couldn't be hearing her mother singing a low, rhythmic song. She couldn't be hearing her father good-naturedly arguing on the phone with a friend overseas.

She inhaled deeply.

The air didn't smell of dust or lavender from the closet's hanging sachet in the room where she fell asleep.

It smelled of noon chai. Not doodh chai, black tea with scalding milk that was the pride of any Bangladeshi family gathering. Noon chai was Kashmiri to the core, and her father was the expert in the family in brewing it: green tea and milk and a pinch of baking soda, outrageously pink and as savory as a samosa, rather than sweet.

She inhaled again.

Even better, it was noon chai with fresh bread on the side, either for dipping or nibbling on its own, to take in all the warmth and the lingering ash of the oven.

There was something special about a full course of scents, rather than one or two served on their own. A loaf of bread or a cup of tea held right under her nose was nice. It would probably make her hungry, even.

But it wouldn't bring stinging tears to the corners of her

eyes as she thought of balancing noon chai and bread on her knee as she sat on the floor and a large hand stroked back her wild curls.

How could these smells find her here?

It was impossible. And Maria did not deal in the impossible, ever.

She was the kid straining her eyes to spot the thin strings actors flew over stages with.

She didn't bother touching gorgeous rugs to see if they might lift off the floor and whisk her away on a magical ride.

She didn't believe in wishing on stars, or fallen eyelashes, or loose teeth, or what everyone said were most powerful: the secret tears smothered in your pillow, when everything was dark and wrong and you needed a miracle.

(She had been there. Done that.

It hadn't worked.)

But somehow, still, it was her parents' house she woke up in: not Lahore, not Islamabad, and definitely not Long Island, New York, USA.

Her nose tickled with the scent of freshly baked and stacked bread, ready to welcome her at the table with her father's blush-pink noon chai, butter that would melt down fingers and be carefully licked away, and an egg or two.

There were always two breakfasts at her parents' house.

Her father would lay out his fare, and then her mother would clear it away to make way for sweet yogurt, fresh roti or paratha, and buttery suji halwa made from farina, Cream of Wheat.

"Two families, two breakfasts," her mother would tease as she sipped her own milky Bangladeshi-style chai.

Maria wouldn't complain. Because two breakfasts meant her parents were there. With her.

She closed her eyes, trying to corral her scattered thoughts. If this was real, why hadn't either of them come upstairs to get her?

She slid to the floor and padded forward. Everything remained the same around her: the sounds, the smells, the sense that if she went to the window, the street—somehow— would rise to meet her with its carts and people and dusty corners.

She reached for the curtain and flung it back.

And there, spread beneath her, was her parents' garden.

The one she remembered the most, the one her grandparents had planted at the back of their house that, whenever he was home, her father lovingly tilled and watered.

Maria's heart caught in her throat.

This had to be a dream.

It could not be real.

Still, she bolted for the door, stumbling over her suitcase—

just a dream—as the noise swelled and became unbearable: her mother's hum, her father's feet pounding against the floorboards in rhythm.

One hand reached out to the doorknob.

What waited for her on the other side?

Maria opened the door. Everything went quiet.

There was the hallway of the Clayborne house as she had seen each day, dim with little shy rays of sunshine from half-cracked doors.

Maria let out a shuddering breath.

It was a dream. Of course it was. But then why did the aroma of noon chai still hang in the air? Was she being haunted?

"Maria?"

Maria let out a very un-Maria squawk and whirled toward the voice. Lyndsay startled back, hand to her chest.

"Are you okay?"

Maria swallowed hard. "Um . . . I . . . I had a bad dream?"

Lyndsay's face softened. "It's rough to be in a strange place. I . . . came up to see if you wanted breakfast. You slept a little late today, and Charlotte's already eaten."

"Breakfast?" Maria's heart pounded. "What's for breakfast?"

If there was some explanation for the smell, the sounds . . .

But Lyndsay's next words deflated it.

"Oh." She blinked, surprised. "Well. I'm glad you're hungry. It's just pancakes, but you can let me know if you want something else."

If Lyndsay hadn't made noon chai . . . Maria swallowed hard, still feeling the phantom sweetness of fresh tea coating the back of her throat.

How had she smelled that breakfast? How had she seen her parents' garden out the bedroom window?

It nagged at her all through breakfast, and even after as she mechanically went about what she should have done days ago: finally unpacking her little suitcase. Lyndsay watched for a few minutes as she tugged out a few worn shalwar kameez, counted her two little pairs of socks, and put aside her one towel to be washed.

"We'll have to go shopping," Lyndsay said worriedly. "That doesn't look like enough at all. And it's still going to be chilly here for a while."

"It wasn't like I had a lot," Maria muttered. She never had— not because her parents and relatives didn't care, but because moving around a lot meant stuff tended to be forgotten, or outgrown. And recently people had been more concerned with getting her to her next stop than noticing how much lighter her suitcase was now.

Besides, it wasn't like she was unpacking the suitcase because she thought she was going to stay here longer. She just wanted to make sure: had she forgotten a little dried flower in one of the pockets, or had one of her aunts slipped her an instant tea packet?

But there was nothing.

Maria decided the dream—or had it been real?—was a sign that she shouldn't give up on the garden.

So how could she get—and learn—all she needed to help it? By dinnertime that evening, she was determined to try, at least. Even though it would involve a most unpleasant thing— asking adults for help.

Without making them suspicious.

The padlock made her sure the garden was one of the places she wasn't supposed to be. And anyway, she wanted it to be hers. Her secret.

Dinner was soup.

At least, that was what Lyndsay said it was.

"Enjoy," she said wearily, plunking Maria's bowl down with the exhausted air of a waitress in a movie. Across the table, Charlotte let out a little croon of pleasure.

"Oh, Lyndsay, thank you. I was hoping that was what I smelled!"

She was?

Maria wrinkled her nose.

The soup smelled like the air after a heavy storm—not the lush scent of grass and dirt, but the wet stench of concrete and pollution that rose from city streets when people weren't quick enough to latch their shutters against it.

Charlotte was already sipping delicately from her spoon. Lyndsay was giving Maria an expectant look. Maria slowly dragged her spoon through the bland-colored mess.

"I think my bowl is bad," she announced, staring at the clots clinging to the metal.

"It's meant to look like that." Lyndsay sighed. "It's potato soup."

"Rotten potato soup."

"Maria." Charlotte lowered her eyebrows in that way that dadimas and naanus all around the world had in common: the look that said they would be Very Disappointed and find a way to make you Very Disappointed in turn, if you weren't careful what you did next.

Maria gingerly took a lick of her spoon.

It was, unsurprisingly, disgusting.

Even Lyndsay didn't look like she was enjoying it. She stirred her bowl, reached for her napkin, fumbled with her glass, and then stirred her bowl again.

Maria eyed Charlotte and Lyndsay. Charlotte was

engrossed in a program on the small, tinny TV screen, something about big mansions and people in frilly Victorian dresses. Lyndsay kept making small circles in her soup bowl.

Maria sloshed her spoon through hers.

Why was it so hard to figure out how to ask? She wasn't even sure *what* to ask.

To give her space in the yard to garden?

She worked out all the arguments in her mind as she stirred her soup. Gardening would keep her occupied. Active. Adults liked to say that kids needed to stay active when they really just wanted those kids out of their hair. She would be beautifying the yard for them.

She thought of the tik-tiki, crawling up the gate, showing her the right place to put in her nail and work it open and step through.

She belonged out there. The house, the garden, they wanted her out there.

She could feel it.

"I'm bored," she said aloud, crossing her arms over her chest.

"We don't announce that at the table," Charlotte responded mildly.

"I thought we don't watch TV at the table either."

Charlotte gave her a look, and then Lyndsay. Lyndsay leaned forward.

"After we're done with dinner, I'm sure you can find something, Maria. Just finish your soup."

"I didn't mean right now. I meant in general. I want something to do."

"Okay." Lyndsay brightened up. "Asra and I were emailing about that. We're still considering your school enrollment since Asra feels she will be back soon, and I didn't want you to go through getting settled and then being pulled out. But I do have an online curriculum in mind, and I was looking through Charlotte's pamphlets too. There is a lovely homeschool co-op that has arranged a day camp with the local nature center, and there are some library programs . . ."

Maria interrupted her before she could break out the informational brochures.

"Not that. Outside. I want to garden."

Charlotte's spoon clattered into her bowl. "What?"

Maria and Lyndsay both startled and looked over at Charlotte. The woman's face had gone even paler than usual. "Whatever gave you the idea to garden?"

"TV," Maria said. TV always seemed like the safest answer.

"I see," Charlotte said. "Well, I'm sorry to disappoint you, but my greenhouse doesn't need an extra set of hands."

"I don't need to work in the greenhouse," Maria said. "I just want to . . . I don't know, get my hands in the earth? Fresh air? Don't grown-ups usually want kids to be interested in stuff like that?"

"Well, yes . . . I mean . . ." Lyndsay blinked, and then rallied. "Of course. It's still a little cold for anything to be planted just yet. But there's no harm in asking Ethan if you could make a little plot in the yard."

Maria glanced at her, surprised. Lyndsay still looked perplexed, but there was an oddly determined look on her face. "If you'd rather stay close to home, there's always online classes to keep you on top of schoolwork. And maybe playing around a bit in the dirt will help you settle in."

Charlotte pursed her lips and then reached for her spoon again.

"We'll see what Ethan says," was all she said, before taking another sip.

Maria looked down into her own bowl, trying to hide her smile.

She could swear that beneath her chair, the floorboards gave a little hum.

Ten

Of course, Maria hadn't intended to wait for Mr. Clayborne's permission before poking around more in the garden. Why should she, when it was obvious no one had visited it in ages?

But she hardly had a foot out into the yard the next day before a voice was calling behind her cheerily.

"Good morning!"

Mimi Rehman, the Cool Girl—apparently ready to appear at a moment's notice—walked up to her, smiling.

"I was hoping you'd be out again!"

Maria raised her eyebrows without a word. What about their previous encounter gave Mimi the idea Maria wanted to see her again, ever?

Then she saw the boy behind Mimi. And her mood soured even further.

"Who is that?"

Her voice was at her sharpest better-for-you-to-turn-tail-and-flee tone. But Mimi only smiled, those dimples peeking out.

"That's my brother, Rick. He's about your age. He wanted to see what you looked like for himself."

The boy waved, a grin nearly identical to Mimi's crossing his face. He had a bright band of freckles across his nose, and light brown curls. He was practically her twin.

"She wouldn't describe you properly," he said. "She just said you were nice and pretty, but that describes, like, ninety-eight percent of the girls she knows."

"It does not!" Mimi scoffed, folding her arms over her chest.

Rick scrunched up his face and cooed in a high-pitched voice. "Oh my gosh, Laurel? Yeah, she's *so* cute and *so* nice! And Mona? *She's* so cute and so nice!"

"Shut up!" Mimi wheeled around to swipe at him, but he backed away, giggling. "You've seen her now! Go home, and take Noodles with you."

"What makes you think Noodles is with me?"

Maria looked between the two of them. What were they talking about?

And then . . . she couldn't help it. She gasped and grabbed Mimi's arm. "What's that?"

Mimi rolled her eyes and sighed, not even turning toward where Maria was staring: the front of Rick's overalls, which were squirming.

"That . . . is Noodles."

After a moment, a little furry head popped up. A ferret head.

Rick stroked it, smiling.

"I guess he wanted to see you too. Say hi, Noodles!"

Maria cringed back. The thing looked a little too much like a mouse for her liking. She wasn't scared of mice. Not at all.

But it was smart to keep a safe distance from them.

Rick waved and headed down the street.

"Thank goodness," Mimi said. "I shouldn't have mentioned that I was heading over here to see if you wanted a tour of the neighborhood, but Ammu asked where I was going."

Maria glowered at this unwanted complication and change to her plans.

"So, a walk?" Mimi prompted when Maria didn't say anything. "I thought it might help since you're staying with your relatives for a while."

"The Claybornes aren't my relatives," Maria blurted.

"They were friends of my parents."

Maria wanted to smack herself. Now Mimi was really going to turn on the Cool Girl attitude: the "oh no, I'm so sorry," the hand on her arm, taking her under her wing and parading her around as the "poor, lonely orphan girl I'm helping out while she's here."

Maria needed to stay on guard.

For a moment, Mimi was quiet. Maria waited for the pity to bloom across her face. For her to open her mouth and say, "What happened to your parents?"

But all she said was, "Oh, okay. Either way, they should be fine with you getting some air."

Maria's jaw dropped.

"So let's show you a bit more of East Misery!"

Mimi linked arms with Maria and tugged her down the sidewalk toward the street. Maria craned her head toward the house. Were Lyndsay and Charlotte watching her being kidnapped?

If they were, it obviously didn't concern them. Not one curtain twitched.

And then the words sank in.

"East Misery?"

"This is East Misery Road." Mimi giggled. "Dates back to original colonizer times or something. I know, it's weird."

Maria didn't know why she didn't dig her heels in right then and there.

But she didn't.

She walked down the street after Mimi, even once she was able to detangle herself from the girl's octopus arms. Hardly any cars trundled by on the tree-lined, one-way road, but whenever one passed, Mimi stopped and waved.

Most slowed down, and the drivers waved back.

One or two honked.

One woman rolled down her window to call, "Give my love to your mom and Rick, Mimi!"

"I will!" Mimi called back, waving wildly.

Maria tried to shrink down into herself. It didn't work.

"The neighbors here are all nice," Mimi said. "There's a neighborhood party every summer that everyone comes to. Well, except the Claybornes. My mom says they used to hang out more when I was little, but I don't remember it."

"Maybe they're not fond of your brother's ferret," Maria said.

Mimi grinned, and then went on to describe Rick's pastimes. Each one made Maria's eyes widen with additional horror. Running around with wild animals he found under people's porches . . . letting the ferret pop out from his overalls to say hi to grocery cashiers . . .

"Everyone knows Rick at this point."

"He sounds unruly," Maria said.

Mimi looked at her face and burst out laughing.

"Oh my gosh, you sounded like a total dadima saying that! That was so cute!"

Maria glowered at the ground.

It wasn't like she was saying it to be grumpy. She was just pointing out a fact.

She hugged her arms tighter and followed as Mimi continued the tour, pointing at the homes with Bangladeshi families.

"Doctors," Mimi confided. "We're kind of the odd ones out because our dad is white and a contractor, and Mom went through, like, one semester of premed before she discovered the joy of gender studies."

Mimi's mom sounded like someone Maria's mom would like.

And that thought stung.

She made a mental note never to cross paths with the woman.

Mimi took Maria far down the street, insisting that they stop to grab two cups of sugar-chalky lemonade from some little kid she knew. The whole way, she chattered: about how she grew up here after her parents moved from New Jersey when she was two, which neighbors gave out the best Halloween candy, even though her family didn't really celebrate it in that way, or how many times Rick had spilled from his bike while learning how to ride it.

Maria wasn't sure what to say to any of it.

So she stayed quiet.

At least they were turned back around in the direction of the Clayborne house now. The ordeal was almost over.

Maria looked up as a shadow fell overhead. A large tree bent gracefully over a fence they were passing.

"Oh, a weeping willow!" Mimi sighed. "I love these. You've probably noticed, but gardens are a big deal around here."

"They are?"

"Oh, yeah." Mimi turned and walked backward, eyes on Maria. "That's why everyone still thinks it's so sad the Claybornes closed up theirs."

"Really?" Maria managed. She hoped her face was straight.

Mimi shrugged. "I don't know all the details, but it's been locked up ever since Mr. Clayborne's first wife died."

Maria wanted to ask more, but as they approached the Clayborne house, she saw Lyndsay standing by the front gate, cupping a phone in her hand.

"Maria!" Lyndsay rushed toward them, relief on her face. "I was wondering where you were . . . oh, is this your friend?"

Mimi smiled and opened her mouth, but Maria spoke up quickly. "I went for a walk, with Mimi."

Was that a crime now?

But Lyndsay just nodded.

"Good, good. I was looking for you because Mr. Clayborne just texted me."

Maria's stomach lurched.

"About letting me garden? What did he say?"

Lyndsay smiled, but she also seemed surprised by what she was about to say.

"You have his permission. He says you can have your little bit of earth."

Eleven

"He really said yes?" Maria asked.

She couldn't believe it. The way Charlotte always talked about her son, it sounded as though he was exactly like her: grouchy, ready to find fault in Maria's every step and hiss to Lyndsay as she left the room, "When I was younger, we were grateful for new opportunities, but that child never can even work up a smile!"

Mimi nudged her from behind. "What's going on?"

Lyndsay smiled politely. "Oh, I'm sorry . . . you're the neighbor's daughter, right? Mahajabeen?"

She didn't pronounce it at all like she was supposed to, but Mimi dimpled anyway.

"Yes, but Mimi works too," Mimi said cheerily. "At least

for this year. I was Bina last year, and I liked that too. I'm just trying to find the right fit."

Lyndsay blinked.

She extended her phone so Maria could read it for herself.

Let the kid garden. It's fine. Keep me updated. Listen to Mom re: where she should dig up. Talk later.

Was it really that easy?

No questions asked?

"Well, I'm sorry to pull Maria away when you're getting to know each other," Lyndsay said, "but we need to pop by Lowe's so she can get some gardening supplies."

"No worries!" Mimi said cheerily. Maria began to follow Lyndsay to the car, still feeling dazed and hopeful all at once, but Mimi grabbed her sleeve. "Oh my gosh, I almost forgot."

A thick card slipped into Maria's hand. Maria stared down at it.

"What is this?"

"You can read it later, but my parents are holding a milaad, and I get to have some friends over. I thought you might want to get to know some more familiar faces."

Maria would rather die.

But she took the card. And said thanks.

She could throw it away later.

Charlotte stood next to the car in icy silence.

Maria could care less what the lady thought of her, but Charlotte being completely set against her would make things more difficult. That was how old auntie types like Charlotte worked: either they were your allies (at least, as long as you behaved yourself and were quiet and polite and so, so grateful to be here instead of the supposedly awful place you came from), or your enemies.

"I'm not sure why she needs tools of her own, or why Ethan thinks it's a good idea to unleash her on the yard," she said finally.

"Well, he did say you could choose the spot," Lyndsay said soothingly.

"What about the space behind your greenhouse?" Maria asked. No way was Charlotte going to put her beside the house, where they'd be watching her every move. She needed to get back into the garden.

"We'll see," Charlotte said. That was what seemed to be her favorite phrase when she was losing the argument.

It was a relief that she didn't get in the car with them.

Lowe's was surreal.

Honestly, every American store looked surreal to Maria, even just from the commercials: they didn't have the jolly bustle and lively heckling of bazaars or sari shops, none of the urgency of the underground stores she wandered through in Jeddah and Madinah in her mother's purposeful wake.

Even in those distant places, there was enough familiarity to make Maria feel confident. There were rules, greetings, and bartering skills that she could follow along with.

But Lowe's was different.

Everyone seemed to have the same quiet intensity and the same uniform: plaid shirts, jeans, grim expressions as they pushed their carts full of porcelain tiles and buckets of concrete mix. The air was thick with the smell of paint and sawed wood, though she could see neither supply from where she stood.

"Ah, that way," Lyndsay murmured, heading toward automatic doors with the sign GARDENING overhead.

They stepped through into a magical world.

At least, it felt magical to Maria.

"Ugh," Lyndsay flinched, fanning herself with one hand. "No matter the time of year, it's always so humid out here."

Maria had never been in a store like this, where the roof was a clear membrane over the entire garden area, and you could feel the sunlight on your head. And there were plants: rows and rows of them.

Everything smelled strongly of dirt and hose water, and she loved it.

"Excuse me," Lyndsay said, flagging down an employee. "Could you lead us to the kids' gardening supplies, if you have any?"

Maria bristled. Like she needed cutesy gloves and little tools.

But she held her tongue as Lyndsay threw a pair of polka-dot gloves in the cart, and then a bright yellow set of tools.

She could scrape off the paint if she had to.

Or just go through Charlotte's tools. After all, Charlotte had said she didn't see the purpose in Maria having her own.

Her mind was more on the garden, waiting for her.

She shuffled behind Lyndsay and the employee, who tucked plants into the cart: carrots, lettuce and little kale seedlings. Lyndsay tossed in some seed packets, too—"just in case"—for beets, and cucumbers, and little reddish radishes that didn't look like the long, white daikon her naanu preferred.

Maria wanted flowers—big, bright ones—and the type of wandering-vined squashes her Bangladeshi family had, but Lyndsay shook her head.

"These are probably good to start with," Lyndsay said. "We'll ask Charlotte, if you aren't sure."

Not on Maria's life.

She stroked the tomato leaves as she passed, while Lyndsay headed toward the checkout line. It took Maria a moment to realize that Lyndsay had pulled a magazine off the rack. There was a brightness in her face that Maria had never seen before.

"What are you looking at?"

Lyndsay snapped the magazine shut.

"Nothing . . . I . . . Maria, give that back!"

Maria already had it in her hands, flipping through. It was just a cooking magazine. Nothing out of the ordinary about it. At least, until she got to the main feature, and nearly dropped it.

"This . . . Lyndsay . . ."

Lyndsay flushed, snatching the magazine back.

"I submitted that piece months ago. It's nice to see they finally ran it."

"You wrote that?"

Lyndsay sighed. "Yes. I did. I told you I was a food writer."

She did. And apparently she really *was* a food writer. Maria didn't realize she'd said it aloud until Lyndsay looked at her with an insulted expression.

"I wasn't making it up! That article was part of this series where I went up to Canada and did research for a feature on First Nations' food traditions, last year."

"Last year? Don't you still write things like that?"

Maria wasn't entirely sure why she was asking, except Lyndsay was different. She didn't look like the anxious woman who scraped together barely edible meals at Charlotte's request and hid in the kitchen afterward.

She looked warmer. More alive.

Lyndsay shook her head. "That type of article requires a lot of travel and research, and more important stuff has been happening lately for Ethan, so it's been better for me to be the one near home. At least that's how it's felt. Let's put this back."

"Don't you want it? Your name's in it."

"They'll send me one." Lyndsay threw a bunch of gardening magazines into the cart. "You need these more."

Maria watched her as she chose another magazine and reminded herself not to feel sorry for Lyndsay. It was hard, though. She looked so defeated, like a snail that poked out of its shell and quickly shrank back in at the first sign of trouble. Like it wasn't worth getting even more hurt than she already was.

On the drive back, Lyndsay's mood seemed to improve, though. She glanced at Maria in the rearview mirror, her face amused.

"You really like those gloves, huh?"

Maria really didn't. They were just surprisingly comfy. She chose not to dignify the comment with a response, and Lyndsay chuckled.

"By the way," Lyndsay said, deliberate disinterest in her

voice. Maria's ears pricked up. Was she going to ask about Mimi, or about Maria's sudden interest in gardening?

But she just asked, "Yesterday, how did you know my dish was becoming congee?"

That was it?

"The aunties back home used to make me spend time in the kitchen and help out," Maria said shortly. It didn't feel necessary to explain that it was to keep her out of trouble, especially when her parents were gone. "They let me taste things, and well . . . congee is pretty close to khichuri, I think."

"Hmm," Lyndsay said.

Something occurred to Maria then.

"What happened to your congee? Why did we have potato soup instead?" she asked, and then remembered she wasn't supposed to sound like she cared.

In the rearview mirror, Lyndsay's lips tightened.

"Charlotte wasn't in the mood for something different," she said. Nothing more needed to be said.

When they pulled into the driveway, Lyndsay simply opened the trunk, then headed toward the house.

Maria stared after her. "I'm supposed to carry all of this by myself?"

"I want to write down a recipe idea I just had," she said. "Be right back."

Maria sullenly wandered out to the backyard. She definitely wasn't going to be dragging all those potted plants and tools out alone.

Charlotte had already been out. Watering her own plants, most likely, as she left behind puddles of damp ground and the faint snaking path of a hose being dragged toward the greenhouse. Maria sidestepped the soggy patches, staring toward the garden gate in the distance.

"How am I going to get all this stuff there without anyone noticing?" she whispered.

As though hearing her grumble and wanting to give her something else to groan about, the wind picked up. The breeze plucked at her dupatta, whipping it about her eyes and threatening to slide it right off her head.

"Ahhh!"

Maria danced in a circle, trying to pull it down.

Her head tilted as it slid back toward her neck, and her eyes moved up the house.

A window on the mysterious third floor was open.

In it was a figure.

A tall, shadowy figure.

Staring down at her.

For a moment, Maria was frozen stiff.

And then the figure disappeared.

Before Maria knew what she was doing, her feet were pounding back toward the door. She barely noted the raised voices in the kitchen—it sounded like Lyndsay was having a tense conversation on the phone—before she headed for the stairs.

She burst onto the third floor.

At first it didn't look like anything had changed. And then, as she stepped forward, there was a creak. A crackle.

A soft squeak for attention.

Here I am.

Maria's heart pounded.

The door to the locked room—the room she'd heard the rabab music from—was open. A sliver of sunlight eased out onto the floorboards.

Maria crept closer and put her face to the open crack.

And an exhalation of air wafted out—

Freshly watered flowers.

The woodsy warmth of an open oven.

Fresh tea balanced on a tray with smile-sweet sugar cubes.

The smell of home was behind that door.

The house was telling her where she needed to go.

Maria swallowed hard, and pushed the door open.

VII ✍ *The Room*

Past the door was a room.
And in the room was
not
much
room.

The floor was layered with
strewn shirts
half-done puzzles
(just one piece out of place
the glimmering eye
out of socket
in a cat's face
so it winked forever
an elaborately painful detail
in a painfully elaborate picture)
withered leaves, shed
from drooping potted plants
and the shrunken quilt
stretched over the bed like old sun-bleached skin.

Maria walked in

picked over and through
trying to find flesh on already cleaned bones.

Every step took her closer
(a blood vessel nearing the heart
feels every tremor of the vein turn into a fierce
pounding
humming
greeting).

Something waited here for Maria.
Beneath the dull and dusty
the ~~withered and shrunken~~
there was life.
Raw.
Green.

She just had to
find it.

Twelve

The sunlight poured into the window, full and strong even though it was getting late in the afternoon. This didn't look anything like the dark, shadowy place she'd imagined, but she was sure she'd seen someone standing there.

Maria shifted her feet uneasily.

All the horror movies she'd ever seen over her cousins' shoulders or accidentally while flipping channels said one thing: America was full of ghosts. Particularly in big, old, unhappy houses.

But then she steeled herself.

Ghosts were not real.

And Maria Latif wasn't a baby.

This was the room she hadn't been able to get into the first day. Now was her chance. Maybe the house was helping her.

So she turned in a circle, trying to see as much of it as she could.

What she saw was a hot mess. Clothes were scattered across the floor. It was odd, though: some were old and moth-eaten, in such a jumble that she couldn't tell if they were meant for grown-ups or kids. But on top of them were new sets of clothing . . . kids' clothing, in sizes close to what she might wear. Why would those be here?

Two sagging bookshelves were crammed with books. Usually that would be an exciting sight, but these had boring, grown-up titles that her dad would have liked: *Orientalism, Slouching Towards Bethlehem, A Doll's House.*

An old wooden chest spilled over with rugs and scarves, and she crept forward to get a closer look. She held one up, her heart aching at the familiar sight.

Yes. It was a janamaz—a prayer rug—still with the faded image of the Kaaba woven in with black and yellow thread.

None of this could belong to Charlotte Clayborne—not after the look she had given Maria when Maria asked Lyndsay for a spare sheet or a pillowcase to pray on her first night there.

Maria could have prayed on the bed, honestly, but that look made it all worth it.

She put the rug back down and shuffled the clothes on

the floor with her foot thoughtfully. They looked rather clean, actually.

And the bed—though the old wooden posts were coming apart and it gave a dangerous creak when she leaned over to press her hand in the middle of the mattress—was covered with messy sheets and a blanket spilling over onto the floor.

Like someone had just pushed it aside to get out of bed.

Why would a bed be messy in a room that no one was in?

"Get a grip, Maria," Maria muttered to herself. "No ghosts, remember?"

Her eyes landed again on the shelf—and she saw something she hadn't noticed before. Pictures. Three pictures, all in tarnished bronze frames.

The middle caught her attention first, because of the person in it: a beautiful young woman. She had dark, flowing hair and a long nose, and maybe—if Maria squinted—she could see a birthmark to the right of her full lips. . . .

Maria gasped, kicking her way past the piles of clothing on the floor to snatch up the portrait. It couldn't be . . .

"Ammu?"

It wasn't.

Now she could see that the nose was longer, in a delicate, elegant way that reminded her of her aunt's favorite Bollywood movie heroines.

The smile too was wider—narrow lips drawing back over teeth that shone as bright as stars. There was no mole next to her lips.

But there were the hint of dimples, just as sweet and kind as Mimi's. And her right hand was resting on her tummy.

Her very round tummy.

A *baby*.

She didn't look anything like a Clayborne. But her picture was here, and not at all dusty, like someone took good care of it.

Something was heavy in this room, like a storm cloud that needed to be wrung out so it would stop brooding and sulking and throwing gray over everyone else's day.

Maria carefully put the picture down.

She didn't believe in ghosts, at all, but that didn't mean she wasn't going to take precautions.

She stared at it for a moment, trying to get her thoughts in order. The woman's face looked so familiar, even though she *knew* it wasn't her mom.

And then her eyes widened.

"Wait."

The picture of her parents in the garden.

The woman next to them was this woman.

It snapped into place.

"You're thinking of the first Mrs. Clayborne," Gillian had tittered behind her hand to Yusra in the airport. And Yusra had flushed.

Because she was gone.

There was a sudden creak of floorboards. Maria startled, whirling around.

"What . . ."

Nothing was there.

Sheepishly she lowered her hands—and caught sight of what laid atop the desk.

"Oh my gosh."

Maria rushed over, her heart pounding.

"No way, no way, no *way*," she breathed.

Sitting on the desk like a king holding court, was a rabab, a Kashmiri instrument: wood gleaming, beautiful and perfect.

This was even more impossible than seeing a ghost.

Why would a rabab be here? This one didn't look like it had been played. It was museum new, the varnish shiny, with not a smear of fingerprints anywhere on it.

It also wasn't a popular or easy-to-locate instrument.

The only reason Maria recognized it was because her father had one from her great-grandfather. It was a prized treasure that her father touched with reverent fingertips and rarely played, and kept in a place of honor to remind himself of his Kashmiri roots.

"The rabab is the refugee king of instruments," he would tell Maria solemnly. "No matter that we had to leave Kashmir, hearing this reminds us of where we came from. Even if we can't go back, its song preserves our home for us."

She wasn't even sure what had happened to his rabab. Maybe one of his friends had taken it. That probably would make him happy.

Maria looked down at the rabab in awe. Carefully, gently, she lifted it up. The familiar weight raised a lump in her throat.

She thought of her house. Her parents.

Everything that was no longer there for her.

She reached down a finger to pluck a string.

An angry voice rang out behind her. "Who are you and what do you think you're doing?"

Maria jumped so hard that she nearly dropped the rabab. She clutched it to her chest and stared at the doorway.

A boy Maria had never seen before stood there.

He was tall—definitely taller than Mimi, even though he looked to be the same age—and thin in the way Phuppo would call lanky. He looked like he hadn't seen a sweet in his life—not a pastry or a kind word.

His dark eyebrows hung together like storm clouds, and

his long brown face was pinched and drawn.

The best thing Maria could think of, in the moment, was one of those old paintings adults were always making a big deal of—how washed-out they looked until someone scrubbed them down to their original layers, or touched them up with a fresh coat of paint.

The brightness was covered by a layer of sad, clinging grime.

This boy wasn't any happier than Maria was.

"Who are you?" he repeated.

"Me?" Maria finally asked, coming back to herself. This wasn't a ghost after all. It was a boy. She knew how to deal with boys. "Who are *you*?"

The boy looked down his nose at her.

"I'm Colin Clayborne, and this is my house."

Colin Clayborne. A memory flashed through Maria's head, of Charlotte at the table in the breakfast nook mentioning how her grandson Colin was away.

How could she have forgotten?

All Maria could do was stare, hardly noticing the clatter of feet and the anxious call of "Maria?" before Lyndsay rushed in.

"Colin! I told you to stay downstairs and wait for your grandmother."

"I didn't feel like it," Colin snapped back, crossing his

arms over his chest. "You already gave me the sermon, didn't you? I'm in big, big trouble. I'm such a disappointment. Can we move on now? I need to clean up this room."

"You're not staying, especially not in this dusty storage room," Lyndsay said. It looked like she was trying her best to be firm, but her voice was shaking too much to make it convincing. Her usually neat-as-a-pin ponytail spilled ink-black hair over her shoulders, and even the little gold hoops in her ears were crooked.

She looked as shocked to see Colin as Maria was.

Colin rolled his eyes. "It's not like I can go back. I told you, they sent me away."

"But you still won't tell me why. What did you do?"

Colin shrugged. "They didn't want me on campus. What else am I supposed to say?"

Maria took in the boy's clenched jaw, the tight glare.

He didn't like Lyndsay. At all.

Maria glanced at Lyndsay, standing there looking so drawn and concerned—not just because the boy was there, but *for* him. What was there to be so hateful over?

And why did it even bother her?

She shifted forward, and Lyndsay turned toward her.

"I'm sorry, Maria. . . ." Lyndsay walked toward her, reaching out for her shoulder.

Maria hated when adults did that, like they had some magical, memory-changing touch that would make her forget everything.

"I meant to come right back out and help you get your tools out of the car. But then Colin was in the kitchen. Just give me a minute."

"What is he doing here?" Maria asked, pointing to Colin.

"Hey!" Colin bristled. "I asked you that first, and you still didn't answer me."

"I don't talk to strangers."

"What . . ." Colin spluttered, but Maria turned back to Lyndsay.

"I thought Mr. Clayborne's son was at some fancy music school."

"He was." Lyndsay sighed. "He's supposed to be. It's . . ."

"What's going on here?"

Lyndsay's shoulders sagged in relief as she turned to face Charlotte.

"Charlotte. Thank goodness you're here."

Charlotte didn't look like she thought it was a good thing at all. Her lips were pursed. She was all dressed up in a way Maria usually didn't see her, in a suit blue as a robin's egg with big gold earrings and a little purse hanging neatly at her side.

"Colin? What on earth are you doing here?"

All of a sudden he didn't seem confident anymore.

"Grandma. I . . ."

"Answer the question, Colin."

Maria could see Colin weighing his options. He slumped, dragged down by the inevitable. "I . . . I got sent home. My head of guidance escorted me here, because . . . well, I . . ."

"Stop whimpering, and stand up straight," Charlotte barked, so that Lyndsay (and, to her own shame, Maria) jumped. "Now, *why*?"

Colin shuffled his feet. "I . . . I shoved someone?"

It sounded uncertain, like he was making up a story as he went. Charlotte's lips thinned.

"You think you shoved someone, or you did?"

"I . . . I did," Colin said quickly. "I shoved him, and then when a teacher tried to get between us, I . . . pushed her hand away."

Lyndsay let out a little sorrowful exhale. Colin didn't look toward her, but his shoulders hunched even more.

"I'm sorry," he whispered.

Charlotte frowned. "I'm so disappointed, Colin. I'm not sure about the other side of your family, but this is not how a Clayborne acts. I hope you'll have a better and more detailed explanation for your father."

The blood drained from Colin's face.

"What? I thought Dad was away . . . Grandma, please?"

His eyes drifted toward her imploringly, but fell on Maria first. The snarl came back to his face and the venom to his voice.

"What are you looking at?"

"Colin," Lyndsay hissed.

"Lyndsay," Charlotte said, stony gaze still on Colin. "Please take Maria and go downstairs. My grandson and I need to talk. Alone."

"I . . ." Unsurprisingly, Lyndsay shrank back. "All right. I'm sorry. Maria, let's go."

"Wait," Colin snapped. He turned to Maria. "Would you put that down?"

Maria grasped the rabab in her hands more tightly. She was very irritated with this strange boy barking orders at her.

"Why?"

"It's not yours and you're going to break it!"

Maria cradled it closer as Colin moved forward, her tight grip making the strings twang.

"Stop it!"

Lyndsay gave Maria a pleading look. Maria finally set it down—though, of course, taking her own good sweet time. After all, now that the room was unlocked, she could come back.

Colin watched with narrowed eyes. "Is anyone going to tell me who she is?"

Lyndsay sighed.

"Colin, this is Maria. She's the daughter of your father's college friends, and . . . well, she's staying here."

"For a week? For a while?"

"For as long as it takes," Lyndsay said wearily. "Maria, let's go, please."

Maria huffed and kept a firm eye on Colin as she walked past him. He eyed her as though she were a wild snake. It made Maria want to actually bite him.

But she didn't. Who knew what he would taste like, as sour and haughty as he was? And besides, it might be too much for Lyndsay, who was waiting in the doorway.

"The head of guidance told me before she hung up that she's not entirely sure what happened, and you haven't shared the whole story," Lyndsay warned Colin. "But she *will* be reaching out once she's given you a chance to explain."

"Whatever," Colin countered. "She doesn't really care. All of them wanted me gone—just like you did. As long as you don't send me back, it doesn't matter anymore."

Charlotte raised her hand to her temples, massaging them.

"Lyndsay," she said softly. With one last look, Lyndsay walked out, holding the door for Maria to follow.

Maria raised her chin a bit as she looked back at Colin—just to make it clear that, unlike Lyndsay, she didn't find him intimidating at all.

"Stay out of my room," he said. "I don't care who you are, or what you're up to, but at least do that."

Maria's blood froze.

What you're up to.

If he had been the shadowy figure in the window . . .

Had he noticed her staring toward the garden gate?

"You—" Maria started, but Charlotte was already closing the door. A final waft of jasmine and hair oil tickled Maria's nose.

Lyndsay put her hands on Maria's shoulders.

"I think we should talk," she said gently.

Great. That was just what Maria needed: half-truths and coaxing apologies.

"About what?" Maria said, crossing her arms over her chest. Stopping here might mean being able to overhear the discussion inside the room, which seemed like it would be more interesting. Unfortunately, though, the old door muffled all sound inside.

She expected Lyndsay to bring up Colin. The way Lyndsay glanced at the door, it seemed like she would. But instead the woman fumbled in her pocket.

"This."

Maria glanced at the paper she brandished. It was the invitation that Mimi had pressed into her hand earlier.

"I found it on the back seat," Lyndsay said. "Maria, why didn't you tell me that Mimi invited you to her family's party?"

On the tip of Maria's tongue were the blissful, sassy words that would make Lyndsay turn away, no longer wanting to deal with her: *Why do I need to tell you anything?*

But then she remembered how Colin had sounded.

"I don't want to go, that's why," Maria mumbled instead.

"Why not?" Lyndsay asked gently. "She seems to like you a lot. You might be able to make a friend."

Was she serious? Why were grown-ups always so intent on people making friends in places they didn't even want them to stay?

"It doesn't matter, okay?" Maria snapped. "She didn't mean it anyway. I didn't say I'd go and it's tomorrow night."

"I do say so."

Maria's head snapped up.

"You . . . you what?"

Lyndsay's face was firm, her hands on her hips. She looked more determined and put together than she had in front of Colin.

"I'm calling Mimi's mom and telling her I'll drop you

off tomorrow evening. I think it'll be good for you, with . . . everything . . . to get out of the house for a bit."

No.

No, it was not *good* for Maria. Not now, when she'd just found the garden and had the tools she needed to start tending it.

Maria shook her head emphatically.

She wasn't going to let Lyndsay win. Not on this.

"I'm not going. You can't make me."

VIII ❧ Would You Rather

It is a game that
    (like all games
    like all idle play
    like everything that does not serve a purpose
        that others with parents
        and houses
        and suitcases only tugged out of closets
        for sun-soaked vacations and
        well-planned travel)
Maria only knows from a distance.

Would you rather
    do this awful thing
    or that?

As if awful, terrible things give you a choice.
As if they don't merely
    appear
    a wrong turn on a steering wheel
    a sickening crack of bone as you walk
    a phone call in the darkest hour of the night.

But now
>as she huffs and puffs while she works
>flings a withered branch
>onto a waiting pile of leaves
she can't help but play it with herself,
ask herself
what else she might do
to get out of what awaits her tonight.

Would you rather put your head
>in a tiger's mouth
or your cheeks
>between an auntie's fingers?

There are no tigers on Long Island.
>But
>if there were
>>Maria isn't sure
>>she wouldn't take her chances
>>on a wide-spread jaw
>>and waiting teeth.

She is not good at parties.
>They are wilder and thicker

than the tiger's den
in the heart of a thick jungle.

She is not good
    with prolonged stares
    pitying smiles
    persistent inquiries

politeness expected and reluctantly given
    only to find that it is
    as hard to break free from
    as a tiger's claws.

Would you rather choke down
    a handful of dirt
    thick and cloying
    as it meets the nervous dampness of your tongue
or have a platter of Bengali mishti
    rich, round sweets
    as colorful as a collection of jewels
pressed upon you
because
    "Of course you want more, sweetheart."
    "Don't be shy."

"Poor thing."
"Probably hasn't had anything so fine in so long."

Maria licks up crumbs
of stray earth
where they coat her lips.

It tastes richer than rice pudding,
lingers on her tongue with a gentle grit
like cinnamon powder
or the remains of a crushed cardamom pod.

It isn't syrupy as a gulab jamun
velvety and giving like chocolate cream.

But it tastes like
freshness
freedom
as many servings as she wants
without someone assuming that her
giddy greed
means she goes without.

If she wouldn't have to leave

her patch of earth
working her as much as she works it
letting her tug out roots and sift rocks without complaint
silently accepting her frustrated huffs
irritated grunts.

She will reach down
take a whole fistful
swallow it down
and ask for seconds.

But

would you really
truly
rather
be here
alone
not considered
not invited
not missed

or

did it make you feel
a little less

alone
to know that someone out there
wants you near?

Maria's hands
still.

Impossible
    that this question
    is harder to answer
    than ones involving wild tigers
    and clumps of dirt.

Thirteen

Maria couldn't believe she had forgotten one of her own rules.

Never fool yourself into thinking an adult is your friend.

She gritted her teeth as she shoved her feet into her shoes and tossed a dupatta over her head. So what if Lyndsay had texted Mr. Clayborne to ask if she could garden?

It wasn't like it was her idea.

And the whole sob story in the checkout line at Lowe's? How could she have, even for a moment, let her heart soften? Just because Lyndsay looked down at that magazine with her heart in her eyes.

So what if she had talked to Maria like they weren't a grown-up and a kid, but actual people having a discussion about magazines and food?

That was how they got you every time.

Every time.

"Just like everyone else," Maria snapped at her reflection. "Don't forget that."

"Maria? Are you ready yet?"

"No!" Maria called back, tugging her dupatta down viciously. "I'll never be ready. So I can't go."

"Maria, I . . ." Lyndsay cracked open the door and then flung it open, eyes wide. She looked Maria up and down, shaking her head.

"No, no. That is not party wear."

"Of course it isn't," Maria said. "It's for war."

"Maria."

Lyndsay reached out, tugging up the black dupatta Maria had chosen and sighing as she took in the heavy boots, long-sleeved black shirt under a black-and-orange kameez, and floppy orange shalwar pants. "Why all these layers?"

"Less for aunties to pinch. And besides, I don't have anything else."

This should have been enough to make Lyndsay stand down. Maria stood confidently, arms folded.

But it wasn't.

"Of course you do." Lyndsay strode over to the closet,

moving Maria out of the way as she flung it open. "I grabbed you a few things from Target this afternoon, remember? You said you liked that purple dress."

"I said that it was okay, and I also said I wasn't going."

"I heard you."

Maria blinked.

This wasn't what Lyndsay was supposed to do at all.

She was supposed to toss up her hands, give up and give in, close the door the way Phuppo would and leave Maria to her own devices—important devices, like reading over her new gardening books and actually figuring out how to . . . well, garden.

"Nothing in there is good enough for a party," Maria tried again. "My aunt just shoved a bunch of my cousins' old dresses in there. And it's late. I'll look weird arriving now."

"I read the invitation," Lyndsay said as she tugged clothes out of the closet. "You're not that late. How about this?"

She held up a red shalwar kameez, glimmering with gold sequins. Maria wrinkled her nose.

"I hate red."

"Okay, well . . ." Lyndsay put it aside on the floor. She held up another: a gaudy yellow top that Phuppo must have packed for Maria out of spite.

"I hate yellow too."

Lyndsay wordlessly reached for the top beneath it. "That's too blue."

Another. "Not blue enough."

Lyndsay closed her eyes.

Maria smirked in satisfaction. But when Lyndsay opened them again, she looked Maria straight in the eye.

"Okay, I'll just pick for you." Lyndsay fished out a top, and a pair of pants, and a dupatta, and slung them over her arm. "Give me a minute to press these."

Maria flopped onto her bed with a groan, smacking her palms against the mattress. Why?

Not even her own mom would have cared about dragging her to a party when she was so set on not going.

No, a voice whispered in Maria's head. *Not true.*

Maria stilled.

When Ammu was alive, she would cross her arms until Maria found an outfit she liked. And then she would tweak it into shape.

Tweak Maria into shape.

She would tug her dupatta off her face, spritz her with some of her prized perfume, pinch her cheeks until they were pink and a little reluctant smile was forming on Maria's face.

"There's my Maria muni," she would coo. There's my Maria jewel.

Maria's heart clenched in her chest. She sat up, roughly wiping her face.

Ugh. This party was already making everything worse. It was already making her sniffle like a big baby. She could go to a party without her ammu hovering over her. She could go to a party without seeing Baba waiting at the door. Especially since they'd always done it without her.

"Here we go," Lyndsay said cheerily, swanning back in with the clothes extended in her hands. "Nice and . . ."

Her voice trailed off as she lowered the clothes and caught sight of Maria's face. "You okay?"

The last thing Maria needed was noodle-spined Lyndsay feeling sorry for her. Nope, nope, nope. She frowned and crossed her arms.

"Like you care."

It was supposed to come out prickly, but it must have fallen flat. Lyndsay's face creased in sympathy.

"Want to talk about it?"

Maria looked at her sideways. "You want to hear it?"

Lyndsay nodded.

Maria leaned forward.

Lyndsay leaned forward.

Very, very slowly, Maria whispered, "I . . . don't . . . want . . . to . . . go . . . to . . . the . . . party."

Lyndsay huffed. "Maria! I thought you . . . oh, never mind. Five minutes. Five. Minutes. Pray if you need to, and get dressed. This will be good for you, especially with . . ."

She pursed her lips, and Maria thought she could hear, for a moment in the silence, the distant screech of a violin being tuned—badly.

Maybe even deliberately badly.

"Just . . . get dressed," Lyndsay finished, wheeling back out the door.

"You're going to regret making me go!" Maria shouted after her. "There's a lot of bad things that can happen, you know!"

"Maria, what bad thing has ever happened at a party?"

It took less than ten minutes for Lyndsay to thoroughly regret that question. One of the best things about being unpleasant? It is easy to think of unpleasant and terrible things.

"A gang of jewel thieves could break in," Maria said as Lyndsay steered her toward the door. "And they could single me out as the one witness they don't want to survive."

"I doubt there are any jewel thieves this side of the Hamptons," Lyndsay said wearily. "Charlotte, we're going."

"Have a good time," Charlotte said.

Maria scowled at her. She looked very cozy in her

bathrobe, freshly painted emerald toes wiggling into the soft carpet beneath her feet.

"She will," Lyndsay said, and closed the door.

May there be nothing good to buy on the shopping channel, Maria wished Charlotte inwardly. *May a bug fall into your tea before you can drink it.*

May your nail polish chip.

"Maria? Get in, please."

Lyndsay tugged open the passenger door and waited. Maria marched past her, arms tightly wound around her waist, and then clambered into the back.

It was the ideal spot to bore a hole into the back of Lyndsay's head with her eyes. Maybe *that* would be enough for her to call this whole thing off.

But Lyndsay just sighed. "Suit yourself."

As she buckled up, Maria muttered, "A plane could crash into their living room. That happens."

"Very rarely, Maria. And it could happen here too."

"Or maybe," Maria added, warming back up, "some rabid cat will find its way through an open window and bite me. Just me. And then I'll have to go to the hospital and I'll die really horribly and you'll be sorry."

Lyndsay leaned forward and fiddled with a knob. The radio turned on, loud and crackly and blaring a combination of guitar and drums that Maria's naanu would have called evil.

It jittered down Maria's nerves.

Noise. She hated noise.

And there would be so much of it surrounding her, in a few minutes.

"All right, here we go."

Lyndsay eased carefully down the narrow road.

Maria kept her gaze out the window, trying to take in the outside rather than let the music keep grating against her bones.

It was late afternoon—the golden hour, that was what her mother called it. The glittering glints of sunlight pooled against the lively green scalps of tall evergreen trees and off the tops of houses like collected rainwater.

It would have been the perfect time to be in the garden, examining and exploring and letting the last droplets of the day soak into her skin and warm her from the outside in.

"Right here," Lyndsay muttered after another minute. "See? Not far away at all."

And it felt like the whole world shifted.

Maria's eyes widened, and she pressed her nose right up to the window. She didn't care about leaving a smudge from the oily tip.

That was Lyndsay's problem.

No. All she could take in was how *green* this end of the neighborhood was.

There were a lot more trees than before: great clusters of them, ones with leaves she hadn't seen before, and some even with small, tight buds clinging to them, waiting for a proper spring to open up and display themselves.

But the gardens were what caught her attention the most.

There were small flower-bed patches with big blossomless stalks, and others that just had little green fingers drawing up out of the earth—like the plants were reaching out a hand to test the air and see if it was warm enough to leave their beds like a human would.

Some houses had weeping willows even grander than the ones in the Clayborne yard, dragging themselves over white arbor gates and spilling into the street.

How would they look later in the season, when they had flowers and more leaves? Maria tried to memorize the differences between trees, so later she could look them up in the gardening magazines Lyndsay had bought her.

Could any of them be the trees, or the flowers, in her garden?

Even if they weren't, they were fascinating. Not one house's yard appeared alike, or neat, or cropped back and cookie-cutter landscaped like those on the road nearer the Claybornes' house.

They were so vibrant and happy.

Was this something she could do too?

"This must be the house here . . . oh, wow . . ."

Lyndsay's voice raised in surprise, and Maria looked up.

Her stomach churned.

The driveway, and the street as far as she could see, was lined with cars. It took her a moment to see the house: low-lying and large, with brick stairs and bright blue curtains framing the windows.

Even more cars were still pulling up, parking, doors opening to let out large families, fathers smoothing down wrinkled kurtas and giving loaded looks to children already tumbling across the lawn, and moms and stooped-over grandmothers snapping out orders and using their heads to shake the ornas out of their faces before shuffling forward with an armful of steaming aluminum trays.

"Is a milaad a wedding celebration?" Lyndsay asked.

"It's a religious thing," Maria said, staring at the kids going in. More than the adults, the sight of them—especially the pink-cheeked, sparkling girls—made her anxious.

She tugged at the hem of her faded kameez. She was going to be a crow among peacocks, and she hated that she cared.

"It's very long and boring," Maria said desperately. "It goes on for hours, and they definitely are going to eat dinner way past bedtime. And it looks like there isn't any parking left."

"I think you're right," Lyndsay responded absently.

She paused in the middle of the street, staring at the large white house the families were filing into.

Maria could see the distant figure of a woman, resplendent in a bright blue sari, smiling and waving and giving tight hugs before leading people inside.

She swallowed hard, and closed her eyes, and thought the strongest, most forceful thought she could to God and the universe.

Please,

please,

PLEASE.

"Oh! Well, it looks like that family might be leaving," Lyndsay said, pointing toward a car slowly drawing out of a narrow space next to the sidewalk. "So I'm going to pull over there and you can jump out. Okay?"

No.

Not okay.

Was this because she'd already clogged up God's attention with those wishes for Charlotte's nails and tea?

"You want me to go in alone?"

Maria didn't mean for those words to pop out of her

mouth, but there they were: stark, desperate, so close to a whine it made her own head hurt.

The thought of braving those stares when she stepped through the door, filing past the uncles with her head down and into the heavily scented lair of the aunties—without a shield in front of her?

No. She couldn't.

"The invite was for you, Maria," Lyndsay pointed out. "Ms. Rehman has my number. When it's time to pick you up, call. Don't worry about how late it is."

"But I . . ."

Before Maria could say anything further, the car door gave way beneath her arm.

Something warm, and firm, and smelling of cardamom and Juicy Fruit gum, enveloped her.

"Maria! You came!"

Of course it was Mimi, beaming from ear to ear so hard that her dimples were two deeply carved grooves in her round brown cheeks.

Maria tried to pull back, but Mimi squeezed her tightly, firmly, as though they were old friends. And before she realized it, somehow Maria was out of the car.

"I was waiting for you!"

Maria gasped for air. Mimi was definitely a lot stronger

than she looked. Mimi finally eased up, though, smiling brightly at Lyndsay.

"Thank you so much for bringing her, Mrs. Clayborne!"

"Absolutely." Lyndsay smiled. She was in full charm mode, her hair brushed back to show off her prim gold hoops. It was disgusting. "Maria's a little nervous, so I hope you can help her feel more comfortable."

"Leave it to me, Mrs. Clayborne," Mimi gushed. "We'll take care of her, and she'll feel right at home."

That sounded ominous to Maria, but Lyndsay looked reassured.

"I know you will." She looked back at Maria. "Have fun, okay?"

Maria's heart stuttered in her chest. She could feel the sweat beading on her forehead. A group of aunties paused by the door to look back at her and whisper.

But before Maria could open her mouth, Lyndsay was waving goodbye.

And then off she went, back down the street, without a second glance.

Leaving Maria behind with the staring partygoers and Mimi.

Mimi, who grabbed her hand and smiled down at her like nothing at all was wrong.

"I'm so glad you showed up," she beamed, shaking Maria's hand in her grasp. "Everyone's so excited to meet you!"

". . . Everyone?"

Maria's stomach, already somewhere near her feet, flopped itself between her toes.

"What do you mean, everyone?"

Mimi's eyes sparkled.

"Everyone. You're like the guest of honor!" She leaned down to Maria's ear. "You'll have fun. You'll see."

And then Mimi was dragging her toward the front door.

And her doom.

Fourteen

Most people don't realize it, but one of the worst things about moving anywhere new—whether it's a new country or a new house or even a new seat—is introducing yourself to all the people surrounding you in that country, or house, or seat, and . . . horror of horrors . . . *getting to know them.*

Maybe there are one or two delightful people who were born under the right star or have fairy godmothers who blessed them with an actual desire to socialize and not have it be awkward and awful, and actually enjoy meeting other people.

Their hands don't get clammy when they have to shake other hands.

Their smiles do not wobble if they are held up too long.

They can even hold eye contact without it feeling like staring directly into the sun.

How wonderful for those horribly blessed people.

For Maria, it never worked that way.

"I really can't stay too long," she insisted as Mimi tugged her up the stairs. She was dimly aware that the living room was curtained off, though she could hear the laughter of men and the exclamations of boys and a soundtrack of loud pops and whirs—probably a video game.

Maria caught a glimpse, through a gap in the curtain, that made her pause briefly. She could see a kind-looking white man with glasses precariously balanced on his nose. He seemed perfectly at home, leaning forward to make a joke in Bengali as the other men laughed. That had to be Mimi's father.

Mimi rolled her eyes and pulled a little more firmly so that Maria had to move with her.

"I'll get them to turn down the sound a bit, don't worry. We girls have my PS4 upstairs with some better stuff than that. Come on!"

"Wait . . . what about your mom? I should thank her for having me!" Maria was grasping at straws, honestly. For once, the thought of an adult was not so dread inducing as the thought of meeting fellow kids.

Fellow girls.

Girls who looked as bright and cheery as the blossoms dripping off the neighbors' trees. Girls who had parents, and their own houses, and didn't have to awkwardly explain why they didn't have either while wearing a drab shalwar kameez and a permanent scowl.

Maria wasn't ashamed of being unpleasant.

But the thought of facing those eyes, those questions, made her sweaty. At least adults quickly left her alone when she pouted and folded her arms and got prickly enough.

No, she definitely would appreciate meeting an auntie right now instead. But Mimi didn't seem to notice.

"Ammu's in the kitchen with all the aunties," she explained. "I don't know about you, but I'm not in the mood to go through the cheek pinching and the asking to see my report card. Come on. She'll probably be up to meet you later."

Before Maria could protest, Mimi was leading her down a lush hallway. The carpet was soft underfoot, and the gentle blue walls were lined with elegant family photos.

The door they were headed for was obvious: cracked open so Maria was already able to hear laughter and squeals.

Her stomach churned.

"Maria's here, guys!" Mimi crowed, pushing Maria through the door first and flouncing in afterward.

All that Maria could take in at first were eyes. Girls filled the room, on the bed and the floor and one even perched very dangerously on the TV stand with her back against the razor-thin screen. But they all turned to look at her.

Stare at her.

Maria tasted metal clawing up her throat.

"Hi!" one of the girls said.

". . . Hi," Maria managed. Or at least, she thought it was her own voice.

"This is Tara," Mimi said, pointing to the girl against the TV. "And her sister, Riya. My friends from school, Laurel and Anne. Amna and Pat are going to be by later. Amna is stuck in traffic and Pat said their parents had some errands to run first. This is my cousin Mona, and my other cousin, Lisa."

Mona and Lisa? The look on Maria's face must have been more telling than she thought, because one of them snorted.

"Ammu's a big da Vinci fan," she explained. "She wrote her thesis on him in college."

Maria nodded as though she knew what a thesis was, but she couldn't think of a thing to say.

The girls glanced up and down, lingering on her frayed sleeves and her tight face. Something about the softness of their smiles and the looks in their eyes set her on edge. She didn't have to worry about them asking about her parents. They already knew.

"I . . ." Maria tried to back up, but Mimi was closing her in.

"Here, take a seat." She patted the bed, next to Lisa—or was it Mona?—and Maria sat, dazed.

"I'm going to get your goody bag from by the door. I'll be back in one second."

"Don't—" Maria started, but Mimi was already gone.

For a moment there was silence. But not the peaceful silence Maria craved. Expectant silence.

Laurel leaned forward.

"So, Maria, are you liking it here so far?"

"Here?"

Was this some sort of trick question? She'd only been in the house for five seconds.

Laurel laughed. It didn't sound like a mean laugh at all: it was soft, like Laurel's long brown braids on either side of her face and the doll she was turning over between her hands. Kind, even.

"The real question is," said Lisa (or was it Mona?), "how are you doing with the Claybornes?"

Laurel shook her head disapprovingly, but Tara popped in, eyes wide. "You're with the Claybornes? Are you Colin's cousin?"

"No," Maria blurted out. "They're . . . family friends." The noise was building, in her ears and right next to her heart. Had it been so hot in the room when she first stepped in?

"At least Mr. Grumpy's off at that music conservatory," Tara said. Mona (or maybe Lisa) snorted in agreement.

"I *wish* he was off at his fancy music school," Maria muttered, before she could stop herself.

Just then Mimi bounced back in with a bag she dumped into Maria's lap. Maria fumbled to catch it before its contents spilled out.

"Wait, Colin's back?" she said.

"Oh, no," Lisa (or Mona) moaned. "Here we go again. You can't be friends with everyone, Mimi. Some people are just too difficult."

Mimi flopped down on the bed.

"I know he can be . . . a lot. But I feel sorry for him, honestly."

"Sorry for him?" Maria wrinkled her nose. She didn't like the sound of that. Was that why Mimi kept trying to draw her in—feeling sorry for her, because she was difficult like Colin?

"His mom died in that house, you know," Mona (or Lisa) said in a hushed voice.

Maria's heart froze. She knew Colin's mother, the first Mrs. Clayborne, had died.

But died in the house?

"Mona, don't scare her like that." Laurel scowled. "It's just a rumor."

"Is not," Mona shot back. "My mom was friends with her. She remembers."

Maria was hardly listening. All of a sudden it was too much.

She pushed herself up, goody bag tumbling from her lap. All eyes instantly landed on her again.

"Hey, you okay?" Laurel asked.

"I'm thirsty," Maria mumbled. "Um, no, I mean, I need the bathroom."

"Oh, I can show you—" Mimi started.

"No! No. I'll find it."

Before they could say anything else, Maria rushed out of the room.

Heart pounding in her chest, she made her way down the stairs and paused near the bottom. She wanted to leave, to be away from noise and eyes. . . .

She should call Lyndsay. She should tell her to come and get her.

The kitchen was, thankfully, empty. She found the phone and then remembered Lyndsay had given her number to Mimi's mom. She leaned up against the cool counter, trying to calm her body.

The aunties in the next room were giggling, but their conversation skipped between Bengali and English in ways she could not follow. Still, it conjured up the memory of lying down as a ceiling fan whirred and her mom's fingers stroked back her hair and the women of her family giggled around her, discussing husbands and children, good recipes and extended families' illnesses.

Maria's heart clenched. There was no way she was going in there.

Who knew how long it would take Lyndsay to come get her—if she came at all, and didn't try to convince Maria to give the party more of a chance?

Besides, she didn't need Lyndsay to pick her up like a baby. She could walk home by herself.

So she did.

She walked down the road, clinging to the far side as the sunlight dimmed and the streetlights winked on like the fireflies she'd gathered at night in Bangladesh. Their glow didn't fill her with any warmth. With every step, the stares of those girls, their gossipy chatter, seeped into her bones. *"Just too difficult." "I feel sorry for him."*

Would they be talking about her too, now that she was gone? Probably.

As she approached the Clayborne manor, her spirits sank

lower. The door opened before she even got to the porch, and Lyndsay was standing there looking worried.

"Maria! Thank goodness. Mimi's mother called and I . . . why did you leave the party?"

"I didn't feel well."

"I told you to call me."

"Well, I told you I didn't want to go!" Maria snapped. "You didn't care, so why would you care if I called?"

She thought Lyndsay would get mad. Instead, the woman's brow furrowed.

"Did something happen? Are you okay?"

"Nothing happened!" Maria balled up her fists. "I . . ."

Before she could say anything else, a scream of rage echoed through the house.

Maria froze.

So did Lyndsay.

And then there was complete silence.

"What was . . . ," Lyndsay started, and then there was another yell.

Lyndsay rushed up the stairs. For a moment Maria just stood there. Then she followed.

Maria burst through the door, on Lyndsay's heels.

Colin was fuming, slamming books off his desk, kicking at the clothing lying on the floor. Charlotte hovered over him.

"It's not broken," she said, holding something out to him. "Just look at it."

"No! It's ruined!"

"Colin, what's . . . ," Lyndsay began.

Colin whirled around. When he caught sight of Maria, his face contorted into a snarl.

"You. You were poking around in my room again, weren't you?"

Maria crossed her arms over her chest. She wasn't scared of this boy. Not one bit. "For your information, I was at a party and just got home."

"Well, you must have done something! Look!" He turned back toward Charlotte and snatched whatever she held, cradling it to his chest. With a start, Maria realized it was the rabab. One of the strings curled back like a cat's cruelly tugged whisker.

"Colin, that's enough," Charlotte said sharply. "A Clayborne doesn't act like this. I told you we could Google someone in music repairs in the morning. You need to calm down."

Colin tuned her out as though she was background TV noise, spouting off a PSA he didn't want to listen to. He looked like a baby, one of those babies Maria really hated the most, that cried all the time and didn't seem happy unless everyone around them was fussing over their blanket and giving them a bottle and kissing their forehead all at once.

His eyes stayed on Maria.

"It's your fault. You shouldn't have touched it. So fix it!"

Now Maria was angry. How dare he bark orders at her!

"I don't have to do anything! You were the one who threw the rabab on the bed because you were so mad I touched it and got my germs on it or whatever!"

Maria chose not to mention the fact that maybe she didn't know *how* to fix a rabab. It was better to let people assume she knew everything.

But Colin looked unmoved, so Maria whipped out her hand toward Lyndsay.

"Your cell phone," she said, putting all the disgust she could muster in her voice.

Warily, Lyndsay handed over her phone. Colin huffed as Maria brought up a video site and typed in a name. Then she shoved the phone at him.

"Here. Watch that."

In it, a solemn-faced, dark-haired, and bearded man was holding a rabab. With a soft Arabic lilt, the man instructed, "Care is the thing here. You must always treat your instruments with care."

After a moment, he reached down and raised a thin string.

Lyndsay turned to look at Maria. "How did you know to look up that man?"

"He's a friend of my dad's," Maria said, and immediately regretted it. *He was, at least.* She hadn't seen Dr. Tayyeb Imran in years, but she could remember the days when he was a fixture on their couch: sipping tea with her father, drawing her close to pinch her cheeks so that she scowled at him (and then he would laugh and pinch them more, annoying man that he was).

"He's an expert on Middle Eastern and South Asian instruments," Maria added loftily, satisfied to see Lyndsay and Colin's awed expressions. "Famous, even."

"Well, then," Charlotte said. "Colin, thank Maria for finding that video for you. You can watch it and fix the rabab after dinner."

"No," Colin snapped. "I want it fixed now."

"Colin," Charlotte forced through gritted teeth, "a Clayborne doesn't—"

"We'll never eat if we do this the Clayborne way," Lyndsay broke in. Everyone looked at her in surprise. She sighed. "Just . . . Maria, please."

Maria gnashed her teeth. "Fine."

She watched the man in the video, then took the string between her fingers. It quivered like a caught butterfly as she inhaled.

Focus.

The string nestled back in place.

Maria shoved it at Colin.

"Good as new. You happy now?"

Now that the rabab was back in his arms, and in one piece, Colin seemed to have found his volume control. "Is a rabab really what it's called?"

"Look it up for yourself. I thought you were some musical genius."

Colin flushed. "I . . . I never have to fix my own instruments. My dad . . . sends money and I . . ."

Maria rolled her eyes. "Oh, so you're not just a baby. You're a spoiled baby."

"I am not!"

Maria turned to Lyndsay.

Lyndsay nodded gratefully. "I'll be right behind you. Thanks, Maria."

"Wait! I didn't say you could leave!" Colin, who had sat down on his bed to stroke the rabab like it was a lost kitten, bolted back up, eyes wide.

"Well, excuse me. Are you the president? A prime minister? Some type of prince? I'm not here for you to order around. It's getting late and I'm hungry."

Maria marched out the door, Lyndsay quietly following.

Charlotte pressed a hand to her head.

"A painkiller, I think," she mumbled, "and bed."

Maria hardly heard her.

She was furious.

What an awful boy.

No, not just awful.

Unpleasant.

She was going to stay away from him as much as possible.

Fifteen

After the night Maria had had, she was expecting gray skies and stormy rumblings to greet her as she woke up.

But everything was surprisingly quiet. Peaceful.

At least, if you ignored the grim expression on Charlotte's face as she buttered her toast. Lyndsay was already holed up in the kitchen, but the dinging and clanking of her pots and pans was more subdued than usual.

There was no sign of Colin, for which Maria was grateful. She ate her own toast and eggs as quickly as possible, and slipped out the door to the yard.

She spent some time in the decoy garden first, half-heartedly clearing away grass with an eye on the window to make sure she wasn't being watched. Once that was done, it was time to head where she actually wanted to be. She was gripping the handle of the garden gate when she heard the voice behind her.

"What are you *doing*?"

Maria nearly jumped out of her skin. Colin was coming around the side of the greenhouse, his eyes on her.

"I'm minding my business, which is what you should be doing," Maria snapped. "And didn't I say I didn't want to talk to you?"

"Trying to look in there isn't your business," Colin Clayborne pointed out. He was annoyingly calm, standing there with his hands in his pockets.

It irritated her when people did that. They never seemed to realize it, how their hands would go to their pockets while they made demands of her. It was so hypocritical: trying to guard their own possessions, while wiggling out her secrets at the same time.

"Are you spying on me?"

That took Colin aback. He blustered.

"I'm not . . . I just . . . came out to see if you wanted lunch."

"Sorry, I don't eat baby food. You can have it all to yourself."

"I'm not a . . ." Colin exhaled. "Look, maybe . . . we got off on the wrong foot."

Maria's eyes narrowed. "The words you're looking for are

'thank' and 'you.' Together. At the same time. And you should have said them last night." Maria let go of the gate and sidled away. She tried to keep a calm face on. Maybe he wouldn't realize she hadn't just been looking, but was about to open the gate.

But Colin's gaze sharpened.

"So what have you been doing out here all morning?"

"Just exploring," Maria said, and then winced. Wasn't that what every spy said in old movies? "I mean, your grandmother gave me a spot to garden by the—"

To her horror, Colin was no longer paying her any attention. His eyes were fixed on the open lock on the garden door.

"Is that unlocked?"

"Wait—" Maria started, but Colin had already reached over to grasp the handle. His lips were thin.

"Did you . . . did you go inside?"

"I . . ."

But before she could decide what to say next, the gate swung open.

Colin rushed in.

Maria followed him. "Stop, you can't—"

Her words crashed into Colin's back, along with . . . well, the rest of her. Because he had come to a sudden, unexpected stop.

"What are you doing?" Maria seethed, rubbing her now aching nose.

But Colin didn't seem to have heard her.

His eyes were wide as he stared around the garden. It didn't look much better than it had when she first walked in, but she thought there were some improvements. Yesterday, before the milaad, she had done some weeding and swept some of the leaves into neat piles.

And there was the sari still wrapped around the bench, waiting for an owner who would never return to fetch it or the mildewing blanket folded next to it.

Colin stared.

And then he spoke quietly.

"I've never been in here. This is my mother's garden."

Maria stared at him.

For once she didn't quite know what to say. Something sharp and snarky felt wrong, even for her.

It was quiet and awkward. Colin didn't seem to mind it, so Maria stared at the tree.

She cleared her throat.

And then snuck a peek at Colin's face.

To her horror, his eyes were wet with tears, his cheeks red and flushed.

"Are you crying?" Maria blurted out.

"No!" Colin snapped back. "What's it to you, anyway?"

"Nothing," Maria sniffed. "I just . . . was wondering."

Colin gave a little wet gurgle in response, so Maria turned back to glare at the tree. Why was he being so weird about it? Didn't he know it was better to act like it didn't bother you, pretend it wasn't a soft spot so people forgot about prodding it? Everyone asked her where her parents were, and she simply gave a stern look to let them know—without saying a word—that it was none of their business.

"If this is your mom's garden, why haven't you ever been inside?"

Colin rubbed his face. "Because I haven't. You think that lock was there for decoration? My father doesn't let anyone in here."

"Not even you?" Maria asked doubtfully.

Colin turned on her, his eyes blazing.

"Listen, you . . . you're not supposed to be in here anyway. This is my house, not yours."

"For your information," Maria said loftily. "I have permission from Mr. Clayborne to garden out here."

Colin's mouth dropped open, which was very satisfying. "Permission . . . from my dad?"

"Yes," said Maria.

If Phuppo could hear her, she would probably pinch her

ear and tell her that God had a special place for liars—and it wasn't a comfy one.

It was a good thing Phuppo was thousands of miles and several countries away.

Besides, it wasn't a complete lie.

Just . . . most of one.

Colin looked at Maria for a moment. It was the type of look that seemed to go through right to the bones, to see if someone was really what they said they are.

It was the type of look Maria usually gave, and having it turned on *her* made her squirmy and uncomfortable.

Finally Colin shrugged.

"Whatever. Typical. Well, I guess it doesn't matter as long as you stay out of my way."

Maria barred his path as he moved toward the bench, her eyes narrowed.

"Wait, what do you mean by that?"

"By what?"

"It sounds like you plan to stay out here."

Colin looked at her as though *she* was the weird one. "Why not?"

"Why . . . I got the permission! If you want your own garden, write your father and ask him for one." She stabbed her finger toward the gate.

"Do you really want me to leave?" Colin sat down, crossing his legs. "I'll just go straight to Lyndsay and tell her that you're out here poking around behind my dad's fence. But that won't matter since you have *permission*, right?"

Maria had thought she knew what it was like to hate someone before now.

But no one else had ever made her feel the way Colin Clayborne and his smug face did.

"Well," she blustered. "Fine. Whatever. But you stay out of *my* way."

Colin frowned and opened his mouth—but then recoiled from something on the seat beside him. "What is *that*?"

"What?"

For a moment, Maria saw nothing but creeping weeds and crumbling wood. She was about to write it off as an overreaction—*really, such an annoying boy*—but then she saw a flicker.

A little flighty movement of green.

"Tik-tiki!" Maria blurted out with delight.

"Tik-*what*?" Colin asked, eyeing it with disgust. Maria wanted to tell him his face would stay that way, but she settled for shoving him aside to offer a hand to the gecko.

"Of course you wouldn't know a tik-tiki when you see one. Here, little one. It's all right."

But the tik-tiki skittered away.

Maria frowned. First it wanted to be friends, and then it didn't want anything to do with her? Well, fine.

There was a slight crunch of leaves. "Uh, Maria?" Colin said, his voice tense.

"Oh, come on, Colin, it's just a lizard," Maria said, turning.

And her stomach dropped.

Two very surprised—and awed—faces stared back at her.

Rick and Mimi stood by the gate.

Sixteen

How had everything spun out of Maria's control so quickly?

She'd only had moments to adjust to Colin's intrusion before Mimi and Rick tumbled in.

That didn't go well at all, at least at first.

"You told them to meet you here?" Colin ranted, pacing back and forth in front of the bench.

"I didn't tell them, but it's not like it's hard to find me," Maria said, her arms folded. "I'm not suspended from some big famous music school, after all. Or a spy. Or something."

"You totally left like a spy, though. I was worried," Mimi interjected. The other girl didn't even shrink under the murderous glare Colin sent her, which didn't impress Maria at all.

Not even a little.

She was more focused on those last words. *"I was worried."*

Did Mimi truly mean that, with all her precious friends and their cool names and attitudes and outfits?

She probably didn't. She couldn't.

"I didn't want to bother you," Maria mumbled. That wasn't any more true than Mimi missing her. Maria Latif didn't worry about bothering people.

Mimi shook her head. "You wouldn't have. I'm sorry. I know I was dashing in and out of the room, trying to make sure everyone had what they needed and then my mom . . . anyway, next time, just tell me."

Next time?

Maria was opening her mouth when Colin's harsh voice broke in again.

"Um, can we focus? I don't care what happened at the party or whatever, but these two being here is a big problem."

"These two?" Mimi snorted. "You could just say our names, Colin. You know them. We were in day care together at Imrana Auntie's house when we were teeny, remember? I bit you once for breaking one of my crayons. We have history. It won't hurt you to say hi."

Colin glowered. "Right now you're trespassing on my property, so watch your mouth."

"Your property? Excuse me, Mr. Fancy Boarding School—oh, wait, you're not there right now, are you?"

Colin shot a look at Maria, who deliberately looked away. She didn't know it was some big secret.

"This garden hasn't been taken care of in a long time." Rick spoke up suddenly, making Maria jump.

Colin narrowed his eyes. "So what?"

Rick just looked at him quietly. Noodles the ferret popped its head out to stare as well.

"We're sorry we barged in like this," Rick said after a moment. "But if you and Maria are going to bring it back to life, you can't do it alone."

Wait, what?

"Wait . . . what?" Mimi blurted out, as though hearing Maria's thoughts. She looked between Colin and Maria. "Are you guys redoing the garden?"

"No," Colin said firmly, as Maria answered, "Yes."

He glared at Maria. "This is my garden, remember?"

"I found the way in, remember?" She turned to Rick. "Are you saying you want to help?"

Rick shrugged. "I like plants. And I help my dadima all the time."

"Yes, we totally love gardening in our family," Mimi gushed, finally catching on to the subject. "Seriously, we can help. Do you have tools? Plants? Tarp? Soil?"

Maria's head was spinning. "I don't know if it's a good idea," she started.

"Why not?" Colin shrugged as she turned her incredulous glance on him. He had a challenging smirk. "You asked permission from my dad, didn't you? Why *wouldn't* it be okay for them to help? You know, if you're telling the truth."

"I asked permission just for me," Maria blustered. "And . . ."

Colin waited. So did Mimi and Rick.

"I . . . may have permission to garden in the yard," she mumbled finally. "Not here, specifically."

"I knew it!" Colin crowed. "I knew it!"

"It's not like you're supposed to be out here either," Maria hissed. "We'll both be in trouble."

"You don't have to be," Rick broke in again. "I'm no snitch. Mimi isn't either—right, apu?"

Mimi nodded earnestly.

Maria was torn. More hands would definitely help her get the garden back to what it was in the picture. And besides, what did she care about getting in trouble? That wasn't new for her.

What could they do, send her away? They were going to do that anyway.

She looked from Colin to Mimi and Rick.

"If you help us," she said slowly, "there have to be rules."

Mimi clapped her hands excitedly, but Colin stared at her. "Are you serious right now?"

"No telling adults about this," Maria spoke over him. "And no friends either. It stays between the four of us."

Mimi and Rick nodded.

"And I'm in charge," Maria added. "Not Colin."

"I *just* told you that this was my garden. I'm a Clayborne, and . . ."

Maria turned on him. "So? What do you want to do? Where do you want to start? What do you want to plant?"

Colin spluttered for a moment, then tossed his hands in the air. Maria was tempted to tell him he looked very much like his grandmother doing that. But that would probably get him talking again.

Mimi cheered, "Yay!" At a look from Maria, she exaggeratedly lowered her voice. "Sorry. I mean, yay. Wow, this is so exciting."

Rick nodded. "Thanks for letting us help."

It wasn't as though Maria really had a choice.

"But," Rick added, "how are you going to keep the adults, like, literally in the house, from knowing about this?"

Maria opened her mouth, and closed it.

That was a good point. It had been easy for one kid to slip

out and disappear into the backyard to tend the patch behind the greenhouse.

"If you have permission for some space at least," Mimi piped up. "Maybe we can say we're helping with that? The more the merrier, right?"

It was so simple that Maria wished she had thought of it first, so Mimi didn't look so pleased with herself. And then Rick made things worse.

"To really sell the story," he said slowly, "I think Colin needs to be out there with you for a few days. After all, why bring anyone else in when you have help in the house?"

Maria's stomach sank.

She didn't like the sound of that.

Of course, since she didn't, Colin absolutely did, which led to the two of them silently working in the fake garden the next day.

"I'm surprised to see the both of you out here," Charlotte called, approaching her greenhouse as Maria and Colin gloomily dug holes in the ground. "Colin, I hope you aren't pushing yourself too hard. You're not usually good with the outdoors. And did you put on any sunscreen? You don't want to get any browner."

Maria narrowed her eyes. She didn't like the way Charlotte's lips curled on the word "browner." Like it was a bad thing.

"I did, okay?" Colin mumbled. "And I don't mind the outdoors, sometimes."

Maria snorted under her breath. Up until Charlotte had made her appearance, she'd had to listen to nonstop whining.

"It's so hot. Why is it so hot right now?"

(Refrigerators were probably warmer. Maria occupied herself for a few blissful moments imagining how Colin would melt away if he were somewhere truly hot—like Lahore, or Jeddah.)

"You want me to do *what* with *this*?"

(Dig a hole with a trowel, but apparently in Colin's world, that was on the same level as being asked to rob a bank.)

Maria wasn't sure why he seemed as wary of his grandmother as she was. They were both so horribly annoying. They should have understood each other perfectly.

Even now, Charlotte tried to coax him again into conversation. "Well, my greenhouse could use some extra hands too."

"I thought—" Maria began, and then closed her mouth under Charlotte's sharp glance her way.

"That's okay, Grandma," Colin said. "I'd rather work here."

"Well, maybe I don't want you to," Charlotte snapped. "Take those earbuds out for a second and come over and talk to me."

Colin yanked his earbuds out with a sour look and followed his grandmother sullenly toward the greenhouse. Maria turned back to her work, fiercely digging into the stiff earth.

She could tell by the look on Charlotte's face exactly what—or who—they would be discussing, and it wasn't the greenhouse or Colin working out here.

". . . Don't waste your time," drifted Charlotte's voice. She could hear Colin, faint and defeated, in response, but not the words.

Maria looked between the trowel and the small, sad garden patch. With a sigh of frustration, she tossed the trowel down.

Fine. Maybe she was curious.

Maria crept as close as she dared to the open greenhouse door. Even from that distance, the place was overwhelming: white floors meeting glass walls and ceiling, with towering spiky plants, swollen tree trunks, and lurid, thick-scented blooms spilling onto the floor.

She felt dizzy breathing it all in.

"She didn't make me help her," Colin was protesting, and Maria held her breath. "I was just curious, that's all."

"You should be curious about your suspension," Charlotte snapped. "I want you to keep up with your studies and write an apology letter to that boy you say you shoved. That would be a better use of your time, Colin—not following after that girl."

"So if it's a waste of time, why aren't you making her do something else?"

Charlotte's teeth audibly clenched. "Because she's not my concern, Colin. You are. You should feel lucky. Maria doesn't have anyone worried enough about her digging in the dirt. There's no one to reprimand her for talking back, or being disrespectful, or wasting her time. When she's too old to do that—well, I guess she'll have to face that when the time comes. But I don't want you to think that she's better off than you. After all, you're a Clayborne. You just need to act like it."

Maria had two urges in that moment.

One was to stalk right up to Charlotte and show her exactly how much Maria was restraining herself on the talking-back-to-people thing.

And the other was, oddly enough, to smack Colin and make him retort to his grandmother. Something like, "My mom used to dig in the dirt, so why can't I?"

Something like, "I don't have to be what you want me to be."

But she didn't.

Because Colin sighed and went, "Okay, Grandma. I'm sorry."

Maria's hand clenched into a fist at her side as she marched back to the patch of earth and took her trowel. As soon as Charlotte left, she was going to take out her irritation on the one remaining straggly patch of grass that needed to be uprooted.

It was fine. She was fine. She and Colin weren't friends. He could bond with his mean old grandma over how much of a brown, brash mess she was all he wanted.

She wasn't going to let Colin Clayborne ruin this for her.

Seventeen

As it turned out, settling into the garden with four people instead of just one involved some . . . growing pains.

Starting with the fact that apparently—as Maria found out within the next few days after their discussion—she couldn't sleep in on the weekends anymore.

That was confirmed the first official day of garden "work" by a tentative, but persistent, tap on her door. Maria ignored it at first. She'd only barely managed to get up to pray her Fajr, and she collapsed right back into bed afterward. The floorboards were too cold, and she was tired.

But eventually she dragged herself to the door. Lyndsay was standing there, looking groggy herself but already with a mug of coffee in her hand.

"Maria," she whispered. "I'm sorry, but Mimi and Rick are here and they say they want to help you out in your garden. Do you want me to invite them in?"

That woke Maria up real fast.

"What were you two thinking?" she hissed at Mimi later, as the other girl blithely held out her plate for two pancakes and beamed at Lyndsay. "And why are you eating breakfast here?"

"Ducked out and told Ammu we would eat with you," Mimi mumbled around her meal, and smiled. "She said to say thanks."

Rick was in on the pancake action too, feeding little nibbles to Noodles and explaining to a rather appalled Charlotte, "He's more of a blueberry guy than a dough guy."

"Imagine that," Charlotte said faintly. That was the one good thing about Mimi and Rick's surprise appearance: between the ferret, and her apparent shock that Rick and Mimi were two brown kids, Charlotte was quieter and more tolerable than she ever was.

They had to wait for Colin to rouse himself. Maria could sympathize with him—and hated it.

"Why are you here so early?" he croaked, scowling at Mimi and Rick.

"The early bird gets the worm," Rick said cheerily.

Mimi rolled her eyes. "He's such a grandpa."

They tromped outside and examined the fake garden plot. Maria could feel Charlotte at the window, sipping her coffee and watching.

Ready to come out if they showed the slightest sign of causing trouble, no doubt.

"This is a good sunny spot, actually," Rick said. "You might have luck planting some vegetables here."

Maria shrugged. She wasn't really invested, but she guessed they would have to think about ways to liven it up too.

Finally they outwaited Charlotte's surveillance. An interesting game show must have come on, or maybe Lyndsay needed hovering over. Either way, she disappeared, and they quickly made tracks for the garden.

As they stepped through the gate, Mimi squealed.

"Oh, this is going to be so beautiful!"

Colin snorted behind her, and Maria narrowed her eyes at him. But he pushed his earbuds in and squatted near a fence, staring hard at the vines trailing up the iron.

Ignoring the rest of them.

Rick walked up to Mimi and Maria, his smile broad and eyes sparkling.

"Okay, so. Let's see what we're working with here."

Maria was all too eager to do that.

They wandered through the garden, examining Maria's previous work. She'd managed to shove most of the dead leaves into piles, so Mimi added to them with her feet and arms, muttering something about needing to bring a rake. Rick looked closely at withered plants.

Maria focused on him. There was a frown on his face, and she was curious—was the garden as wrong-feeling to him as it was to her?

Soon enough, he stopped and tilted his head to one side.

"Something isn't right here."

"What?" Maria asked breathlessly.

"I don't know . . . the garden doesn't match what I heard about from Dadima. There's a lot of dead flowers here, and considering how long the garden's been shut up, they seem . . . too new. And it's a weird jumble of flowers from different seasons too. No wonder they all died so fast."

Relief billowed in Maria's chest. She wasn't imagining it.

She turned to look at Mimi and was startled to find Colin standing there, staring at the ground. Maria expected him to scoff, but to her surprise, he asked, "Do you know which ones are wrong?"

"Colin?" Maria asked, but he was focused on Rick.

Rick shrugged. "Look at this one." He held up a withering stem. "This is an orchid. According to Dadima, they are one of the hardest flowers to take care of. It probably should be in the greenhouse. And this . . ."

He held up another one.

"I don't even know what this one was, but the stem tells me it was also a flower. Probably a really delicate one that shriveled up the moment it got cold. It's like someone was out here trying to keep the garden going, but didn't know what they should be planting, or how to choose. They went for really pretty flowers that die very easily."

"That's odd," Mimi mused. "Colin, have you ever seen anyone coming out to take care of this place after . . . I mean . . . well . . . your mom . . ."

But Colin was scowling. "I don't know," he bit out. And then he walked away.

"Touchy," Mimi whispered. Maria looked at her with a little prick of annoyance. Weren't Cool Girls supposed to be caring about others' feelings? How could she not expect that Colin would get like that when his dead mom was mentioned?

Then Rick clapped his hands together, making them both startle.

"Yep, that has to be it. Someone put plants here that the original gardener didn't intend. And a lot of them look like flowers from a particular place."

"A particular place?" Mimi asked.

"Home," Maria whispered. When Mimi looked at her, she said, "I mean. These were Desi flowers, right? From back home."

Rick nodded. "I think so."

"Mrs. Clayborne was from India," Mimi broke in. "So you think she might have been trying to bring some plants she was familiar with and grow them here?"

"These are too new to be hers," Rick pointed out. "Maybe she had some here, and someone else was trying to keep it going after . . . well, anyway. That may be it."

It still didn't feel right to Maria.

The photo showed the tree in bloom, and she'd seen beautiful flowering gardens back home in Pakistan and Bangladesh. But even more than the flowering gardens, everyone's mom and aunt were into vegetable gardens—ones they could step out into in the morning to gather the evening's dinner.

Why wouldn't Mrs. Clayborne do that, instead of plants that easily withered under the oppressive American chill?

"Well," Rick said, not noticing Maria's silence, "it's good to know what was here." He called to Colin. "Hey, Colin! Do you think your dad might . . ."

Colin stomped toward him, eyebrows furrowed. "Look.

We don't ask my dad anything," he snapped. "If you want to work here, that's the big rule. Okay?"

"Colin," Maria snapped, but Rick raised his hand and shook his head.

"All right, dude. Fine. It's okay."

Colin stormed off. Mimi and Rick exchanged glances, and Maria sighed. She wasn't sure how this was going to go. She wasn't even sure if Rick and Mimi would show up again. But she surprised herself by wanting them to.

She wanted the garden to have hope.

When the sun was high and warm, Rick and Mimi excused themselves for lunch ("Leftover biryani still because Ammu *had* to cook for an army," Mimi moaned), and Colin headed toward the house without a word. With a sigh, Maria left the gate looking as undisturbed as possible and followed.

". . . so nice to see you." Voices drifted toward her as she approached the kitchen door, setting her on high alert. She slowed down, trying to get hold of her nerves, before emerging into view.

"Oh!" Lyndsay said, surprised, then turned to her companion. Maria had been expecting Charlotte, but it was a woman she'd never seen before: tall and willowy, with long dark locs and a queenly expression. "Nidi, this is Maria, the family friend who is staying with us."

"A pleasure," the woman said, like Maria was an adult.

Maria liked her instantly. That hardly ever happened.

"Maria," Lyndsay said, "this is my good friend Nidi. We worked together at a food magazine in college, and now she's the editor in chief."

Maria nodded, unsure how to respond.

"Lyndsay always likes to make me sound super impressive and professional and scary," Nidi said, "but I'm just here to bully her into a feature. You know, she writes amazing pieces."

"I saw one, in a magazine," Maria blurted out, and instantly regretted it when Lyndsay gave her one of those tentative does-this-mean-we-are-friends? smiles. "It was okay," she tacked on as an afterthought.

Nidi smiled. "I see."

She turned to Lyndsay. "I know you and your mother-in-law mentioned that you're busy holding down the fort while Ethan's away, but just one piece wouldn't hurt, would it?"

Lyndsay rolled her eyes. "Charlotte wouldn't mind, but she'd probably try to pester me about how I can mention the great Clayborne family cuisine or estate in some way. Besides, Nidi, I haven't written in months. I'm not sure what to write about, even."

Nidi looked at Maria and smiled. "Maybe company will help you come up with new ideas."

She and Lyndsay walked down the driveway, and Maria turned toward the house, focused on those closing words even if they weren't meant for her.

She had work to do.

And maybe, just this once, Maria needed helping hands to get it done.

IX ❧ *Lonely Days*

Maria has always been
(will always be)
an only child.

"That's why you're so prickly,"
her aunt would sniff.
"Being a big sister softens a girl.
It makes her realize what it means to
share
to
smile
to *be a good example*."

Maria wasn't sure
how *that* was supposed to make her feel sorry
she missed out on the experience.

But she thinks she can understand
just a little
when it comes to sharing the garden . . .

going from having it to herself
(like a mother's lap, welcoming and so nice to snuggle in)
to being jostled by these new eager bodies
raised voices
insistence on attention.

She doesn't think she's gotten any softer
the way Phuppo always ominously promised
though she does find herself dispensing tools
and being asked to check on progress
and
(with heavy sighs)
playing peacemaker on Colin's behalf.

And on the quieter days
the days when she has the garden to herself
it feels different.

More precious in a way
        (because she doesn't have to ask politely

to sit in this patch
and start in on the weeds
or settle over there
because maybe someone else has settled there
and has every right
to enjoy their snuggle
in the warm, welcoming lap of the earth).

But
    maybe
    just a little
    (quieter)
    (different)
    lonely.

Not that she would ever admit it.

Not when she can proudly tell them
"See how much I did without you all underfoot?"
And see Rick's wrinkled-nose grin
and Mimi's affectionate eye-roll
and Colin just scowling as Colin does

and allow herself to feel overwhelmed
and prickly.

Because,
as though she were a burr,
it just makes them stick around her even closer.

Eighteen

"Why are we dragging our feet with this?"

Maria looked up, blinking sweat out of her eyes. It was probably a good thing that she was breathless after dragging the bench farther back toward the trees so they had more space.

Otherwise, she might have bitten Colin Clayborne's head off.

"What do you mean?" panted Mimi beside her. After a moment of gulping air, she forced out, "It's not like you've been doing much today."

"I've done my part!" Colin snapped back. His arms were crossed and he had a tetchy look on his face. "You told me to figure out where those weird greens should go, right?"

"The kale?"

"Whatever!"

"Colin, that was an hour ago." Mimi sighed. "Anyway, look how much progress we've made."

Mimi flapped her arm toward the space around them.

Maria had to agree with her for once. Mimi and Rick had come over every day after school. The leaves had all been bagged and dragged over to line up in front of Mimi's house— "Do you want to explain to Charlotte Clayborne why there are leaves in front of her house? Because I don't!"—and several beds had been weeded and plants identified.

The garden definitely wasn't anywhere near done, but they *were* making progress—and Maria even got some mornings to herself while Rick and Mimi were at school. Colin was still not allowed back on his conservatory campus, but apparently the apology letters Charlotte insisted on did the trick. Every week, he received emailed packets of homework from his teachers, which he holed up in his room to complete most mornings.

Maria was still curious about that whole mess. Colin seemed to have a different story each time Lyndsay or Charlotte pressed him for more details about his being sent home—and none of them sounded quite right to Maria. He always looked a little too cagey to be trustworthy, or else unsure, like he was planting a story in their minds to bloom into the appropriate conclusions, rather than telling them the truth as it had happened.

But she would never ask. That was Colin's problem, and she had plenty of her own.

A flicker of movement caught Maria's eye, and she gasped.

"Was that a mouse?"

She stumbled back, stabbing a finger toward one of the shrubs near the back fence. She had anticipated a bird or something when the shrubs started rustling, but the creature that scrabbled up a branch and vanished looked suspiciously rodenty.

Rick looked up from where he and Noodles were sifting through a tuft of tall weeds.

"Probably," he said mildly. "That's a good thing, right?"

Maria stared at him. "What? No, it's not. Mice are gross."

"Mice are supposed to be outside," he pointed out. "When they are inside, you have a problem. But it isn't a problem to see one where it should be."

Maria opened her mouth, and then closed it.

That was a good point.

"Anyway," he said, lifting himself off the ground, "it's good to have some wildlife back in here. More than one can be a problem when we start planting the kale, so we'll keep an eye out."

"When *are* we going to plant something?" Colin whined. "This place still looks dead. I thought we were supposed to be growing things."

Maria narrowed her eyes at Colin as he plopped down next to her, his earbud cord tossed carelessly around his neck. His hands were barely dirty. Why was he complaining? "Are you volunteering to do it?"

"Yeah, if it gets done."

Maria was about to snap back, but Rick spoke instead.

"I don't see any harm in starting to plant some things. After all, we do have the kale, lettuce, radishes, and carrots that Lyndsay got for Maria, all lined up and waiting next to the greenhouse."

Rick agreed with Maria that it made more sense for the garden to have vegetables than flowers. She wasn't sure why the delicate flowers were there to begin with, but she was determined to move forward with more sensible plants.

After all, those would flower too. She would still get a glimpse of that bright, lush garden her parents were sitting in. She knew it.

"We can try and see what happens," Rick finished.

Colin shot Maria a smug, triumphant look.

"Okay then," Mimi said. "Colin, weed that bed over by the fence so we have some space to put the new plants in."

"Why me?"

"You suggested it."

Colin shoved his earbuds back in, and Maria rolled her eyes. Mimi, though, was watching him with an amused smile on her face.

"It's funny," Mimi said. "I thought you guys would be at each other's throats, but when you're around, he seems a little less . . . grouchy."

"That's news to me," Maria grumbled. As though he could hear her, Colin glanced up. She pulled a face at him. *Mind your business.*

He looked away.

"Oh, come on," Mimi chided. "Don't be like that. He just wants to join in."

"Really? Or was he sulking that we're over here talking while he's working hard at not working?"

Rather than weeding, Colin was peering at the patch with a frown on his face. It was hard to tell whether the frown was for the garden patch, or whatever he was listening to. His fingers seemed to trace out figures in the air—musical notes, maybe. Maria never saw him practicing, but she could hear it in the early evenings: sullen-sounding, thoroughly unhappy pieces that made Charlotte frown and turn up the TV a little higher.

Lyndsay'd had a frown of her own for him earlier. "Will you have those in your ears the whole time you all are hanging out?"

The look Colin gave her was vicious, so she turned her attention to Maria, asking if Rick and Mimi were going to need snacks. Even Maria had to admit that Lyndsay's food was getting better and better now that she was following her own cravings. "I felt in the mood for my mom's beef noodle soup, since it's so cold out," she might say one day. Or, "You wanted a sandwich, Charlotte, so I whipped up some banh mis."

Also, it distracted Lyndsay from asking too many questions. Maybe it was relief that both her erstwhile charges were out of her hair, but Lyndsay adjusted very quickly to the idea of Colin, Maria, Rick, and Mimi being a group of friends and all of them—incredibly—having such enthusiasm for "Maria's little garden project."

If Maria weren't so grateful for her guardian's lack of attention, she'd be a little irritated at Lyndsay's not reading the situation properly—particularly as Colin could hardly be in the same room as Rick and Mimi without rolling his eyes and fuming in the opposite direction.

Rick was very tolerant of it.

"It's okay." He waved a hand dismissively. "My dad says you have to be high-strung to understand the stringed instruments you handle. He's a violinist, right? That's a lot of pressure."

Maria wasn't sure where Rick got his endless optimism from, particularly in the face of a scowling, beady-eyed Colin Clayborne. But she was starting to appreciate it.

And envy it.

Maria tugged at one of the stalks in front of her.

"Colin isn't as sulky as you think. Well . . ." Mimi smirked at the look Maria gave her. "Okay. He is. But not all the time. He's pretty smart and good at sports too. Everyone was always trying to get him on the volleyball team, because he's tall and he's got good aim, but his dad insisted that he focus on music. And since he only has one parent, it made sense that he always tried to make his dad happy. . . ."

Mimi's voice trailed off, the mood lowering with the solemn subject.

In her garden, it felt wrong to gossip about Colin's mom—or ask too many questions—but Maria couldn't resist . . .

"Do you know?" she asked softly. "How she died, or anything about her? Colin doesn't like to talk about her."

Mimi shook her head.

"I'm not sure Colin knows. My mom told me to be careful because Mr. Clayborne's sensitive and doesn't like Colin to hear too much about her unless he's the one saying it."

"So he's still grieving?"

For some reason, Maria felt a pang in her heart for Lyndsay—married to a guy who was still thinking about the wife who was gone. What did that feel like?

Adults' lives were more complicated than she'd thought.

"I don't know," Mimi said softly. "From what I heard, she was really delicate. My mom doesn't really like to talk too much about her either, but she says that they were always worried about her."

Mimi said it so matter-of-factly, but to Maria it was heavy to talk about how someone died. Didn't it bother Mimi?

As though she had heard Maria's thoughts, Mimi shuddered. "It's pretty sad, now that I think about it."

Maria glanced over at Colin, still poking at his row of plants but not quite pulling them up. Did he remember anything about his mom at all?

"I guess I can understand why Colin's dad is so protective," Mimi said, picking her train of thought back up. "And why he always treats him like he's going to break."

Maria frowned. If Colin's dad was so overprotective, why was he away from home so often? When he called Lyndsay about Colin, it never seemed like he even wanted to talk to him.

And then there was how . . . scared Colin seemed of his father whenever his name came up.

"He doesn't look like spun glass, though," Maria said grouchily. "He always has enough energy to cause trouble."

Mimi laughed. The sound of it, bright and beaming like a ray of sunshine almost made Maria's lips tug up too. Almost.

"What a grumpy little auntie. You're so cute, Maria." Mimi laughed. Maria didn't laugh with her. But the corners of her mouth lifted. Just a bit.

Maybe eventually the garden would lift Colin's mood as much as it lifted hers, and he wouldn't be such a storm cloud. Not that she cared.

It was a perfect, mild spring day, the type she was really starting to appreciate, even if the cold breeze off the Long Island Sound and the nearby lake could put a chill in the air.

Usually it was hard to tell that there was something alive but dormant at the heart of the garden—but today, it was everywhere, and as much as Maria basked in it, it also pierced her heart through with anxiety.

How long was she going to be able to soak this in before she was boxed in by Manhattan buildings? She knew Lyndsay stayed in touch with Asra, from her absentminded remarks: "Oh, Asra said to tell you hi. Her mom seems to be doing pretty good" or "Asra mentioned that you might know how to describe the flavor of firni to me."

It was absolutely fine with Maria that Asra seemed to have

no interest in talking to her. But the frequency of her calls still made Maria uneasy.

What if she came back before the garden bloomed?

"Look at this!" Rick crowed cheerfully, holding out his clasped hands.

Mimi leaned in eagerly, and Maria, shaken from her thoughts, followed—only for the older girl to recoil, eyes horrified.

"Oh my gosh, Rick, don't do that to me!"

"It's just a granddaddy longlegs," Rick said sensibly, letting the docile arachnid crawl up his arm. "Wanna touch it?"

"No, no, and no. Ugh."

Maria, though, gingerly held out her palm.

"I don't want it going up my sleeve."

"He won't. Just . . . make your hand a little flatter."

Maria stared down at the large creature as it crawled onto her palm. Her skin tickled, and she laughed.

"Wow! It's . . . not running away."

"They are pretty chill," Rick said, taking it back and gently setting it on the fence. "All right, buddy, off you go."

"No, wait!" Maria turned to look for Colin. She wasn't sure why. Maybe it was the sun, warming her up.

Maybe, if she was in a good mood, Mr. Grumpypants should be as well.

He was looking up at her and Rick, a frown on his face.

"Colin! Do you want to see this?"

"I've seen those things before," Colin snapped. "Mimi's right. They are gross."

Why did she even bother?

Rick looked at her sympathetically. "It's fine," he said.

Maria sniffed. "Do I look like I care?"

"No," said Rick. "Oh, wait. Hey. Look what I found over here."

Maria and Mimi followed curiously to one of the back corners. Rick spread his hand over a little patch of green plants that looked mildly familiar to Maria's eyes: rounded leaves with little grooves in them, and a pleasant smell that reached her nose as soon as she bent down.

"It's mint!" Mimi exclaimed. "And it's super fresh."

"Mint is kind of hard to kill once it gets its roots into the ground," Rick said. "At least that's what Dadima says."

Maria wasn't sure why she thought of Lyndsay as she smelled the leaves, but for some reason, she found herself carrying a clump of mint with her when she pushed through the kitchen door.

Lyndsay was rummaging through the cabinets. She looked up, her brow furrowed, and then sniffed.

"Is that mint?"

Maria held it out. Lyndsay wrinkled her nose.

"Wow. It's gotten . . . a little crushed."

Maria's cheeks flushed. "Well, if you don't want it . . ."

Lyndsay's eyes widened and she reached back out. "No, no! I want. Thank you, Maria . . . where did you get this?"

Maria's tongue froze for a moment.

"Um . . . it came up in my garden by the greenhouse?"

"Really?" Lyndsay's eyes narrowed. But then she shrugged. "Maybe Charlotte planted it at some point. This stuff can really run wild. Anyway, thank you. I'll make some tea with this."

Maria couldn't control her wince even if she wanted to. Lyndsay laughed, a startled little sound, as though she didn't mean to laugh.

"Goodness, tell me how you really feel, Maria. You really dislike my tea that much?"

"It's brewed too long," Maria said. "It's gross."

"Brewed too long? Huh. Well, I'll work on that. You know, my grandma used to live on a tea farm when she was in Taiwan. I haven't thought about that for years, but she used to tell me so much about tea. I probably have that written down somewhere, I'm sure."

Lyndsay wandered off, mumbling about more research to herself. Maria stumbled toward the steps, intent on throwing herself onto her bed. She felt hopeful, even under the bone-tiredness, though.

It was hard not to, when the house soothed her as she went: hallway nightlights flicking on like stars, the carpet outside her room as soft under her bare feet as spring grass, and the pillow letting out a little puff of her mom's jasmine perfume as she laid down her head.

It was pleased with her. She could tell. The grit of soil between her toes, where the garden still clung to her, made it hopeful too.

Tomorrow they would see how the plants they put in today had fared.

Tomorrow was going to be another adventure.

She didn't know then that instead, it would be a disaster.

X ❧ Cold Snap

In the presence of death

    Maria knows she is
    they are

in the company of the

        no longer living
        gone in their prime
        lost but not forgotten
        gone
        gone

        gone.

For a moment, she is no longer standing at a garden gate
    but in the basement of a masjid
    tables still unfolded
    chairs pulled away
    expectantly, like she is entering for a wedding
    instead of a final goodbye.

For a moment, it is not Mimi's hand on her shoulder
but her aunt's
her uncle's
her cousin's
someone's warm fingers curled where bare skin parts with
fabric.

    (She is not sure what she was wearing
    as much as she isn't sure who was responsible for
    holding her down
    keeping her here
    the way they always did
    when her parents asked
    the way they always had
    when her parents left.)

In front of her, neat rows of peppers
parsnips
hopeful carrot tops
droop

and she is steered toward them
by the hand on her shoulder

steered toward death
like she was that day.

Not coffins now
not drawn, familiar faces and folded hands
as though joining in their own janazah.

But still
(sickeningly)
(awfully)

    dearly departed
    preceding us
    moving on
    passing away

gone
gone

g o n e.

Nineteen

At the entrance of the garden, all Maria could do was stare.

The plants, in the neat rows Maria and Mimi had dug with a little trowel and a lot of determination, were drooping and shriveled. Some of them were still faintly green, but with sickly pale tops and dark blotchy spots, as though the cold air had literally taken bites out of them.

"What happened?" Maria whispered, leaning down to take a radish's browning sprout in her hand. It peeled away into her grip, the plant trembling.

"There was a cold snap last night," Rick said grimly. "I saw frost on the windows when I woke up."

Maria had too. The delicate swirls—as though some

teeny, unseen creature had ice skated across the glass—were so beautiful. So pure.

But its effect on the plants was disastrous.

Maria's heart sank as she took in the wilting stems, withering leaves, and trembling buds.

"But the buds . . . they are closed, so they're okay?"

Rather than answer, Rick reached out and snapped one off the nearest plant.

He used his nail to rip open the bud. Inside was a brown, misshapen mass. What should have been bright petals was nothing more than pulpy rot.

"We might not be able to tell," Rick said, his voice still solemn—too solemn. "Until later in the season. Even ones that look okay right now might be damaged."

"But yesterday you said it wasn't a bad idea to put in the plants!" Colin groused behind Maria. "Now look at everything! What was the point?"

"It's been so warm recently, I thought it'd be fine," Rick said, "but I guess that was my mistake."

"Your mistake?" Colin demanded tightly. "The garden is dead, Rick. Dead. What are we going to do now?"

"Colin! Stop it!" Mimi snapped, rushing forward. She tried to grab Colin's arm, but he shook her off, still glaring at Rick.

"Well, Rick? What now?"

"I . . ." Rick seemed at a loss for words. Noodles peered cautiously out the front of his overalls.

It seemed to surprise all of them when a voice broke in.

"He didn't say everything was dead."

It took Maria a moment to realize it was her own voice. Colin glowered.

"What?"

"You heard me. It's not like Rick controls the weather, Colin. We can save them." She looked at Rick. "Can't we?"

Colin opened his mouth to retort, but Rick nodded. "I mean, not all of them, but we can definitely do damage control. Let's cover up the lettuce and kale with tarps for now. You had some potted carrot seedlings waiting next to the patch behind the greenhouse, right? Those need to go inside where it's warm, and from now on, we store anything unplanted under tarps too."

Maria exhaled, relief trickling with air into her lungs.

The garden isn't ruined.

As though reading her mind, Rick smiled reassuringly. "It's still early in the season. This stuff happens. At least we have time to keep planting things that will have a fighting chance."

Colin bent down, examining a kale leaf. "Whatever." He

shook it at Rick and Maria, before letting it drop. "If you guys want to try and salvage a bunch of dead things all over again, go ahead. I'm done."

"Can you calm down, Colin?" Mimi demanded. She kept her hand extended between Colin and Maria, but Maria could see it was trembling. She thought it was nervousness until the girl's next words. "Or are you freaking out because you know this is your fault?"

"Excuse me?" Colin demanded.

"You heard me." Mimi folded her arms. "If you hadn't thrown that little tantrum yesterday, we would've missed this sudden chill entirely."

"I didn't make you do anything," Colin shot back.

Anger flared through Maria. "What's your problem, Colin? Those kale leaves are still on the stem, and it's not that awful black like that other one in the row. The cold tried to kill it, but it's stronger. The garden still has a chance."

"Why do you care so much anyway?" Colin snapped. "It's not your garden! It's mine. I'll still be here and have to deal with my dad and how angry he'll be that we were in here at all, and you'll be . . ."

His voice trailed off.

You'll be gone.

The unspoken words slapped Maria like an open palm.

"Oh," she said. "Oh."

"Maria . . . ," Colin started. Regret washed over his face. Apparently, he could still feel that. "I . . ."

Maria stood, and felt a little sharp sting of satisfaction when Colin flinched. *Good.*

He should feel just as skin-crawlingly wrong as he'd made her feel by reminding her that she was on borrowed time, in a home that wasn't hers.

"Where are you going?"

"Time to get to work," she said shortly. "No matter what you think about these plants, I think they can be saved. And so do Mimi and Rick."

She turned to the two silent siblings. "Right?"

Mimi and Rick nodded.

"So I'm going to walk home with them, and get some more tarps to cover these plants, and you can go right inside and sulk like the big baby you are. Don't worry, you don't have to come back. We can get in trouble all by ourselves."

Mimi and Rick watched her as she stomped to the gate.

"You guys coming or what?"

"We're coming," Rick said.

The gate swung closed on Colin's surprised face. But he hadn't moved.

She fumed as they walked up the street, Mimi and Rick

whispering behind her. She fumed as they found the tarps and carried them back.

And she fumed as they spread them over the plants.

How could she have thought that she might be able to tolerate Colin at all?

She stepped forward, still grumbling to herself, squatting over the kale plant Colin had examined. She brushed the frost off its leaves. The chill stung her fingers, which were already tingling from the cold air.

A little blur out of the corner of her eye caught her attention.

"Tik-tiki!"

The little house gecko was curled in a sorry, shivering heap of legs and tail.

"Oh, you must be freezing!"

She held out her hand, and it slowly crawled on. She tucked it into her pocket, eyes stinging. How could she have forgotten all about it?

She was done trying to help Colin.

She had to focus on this garden and making sure it survived.

That was all that mattered.

XI ❧ Colin

Maria is always the subject of a testimonial,
but has never given one.
This is the one she would offer for Colin
    (if asked).

He's tall.

I guess.

People seem to like it when boys are tall.
    (They never do when girls are
    or at least
    when I am
    stick-straight and unbending.
    It is never a good thing
    a likeable thing
    a   here-is-a-child-who-won't-be-knocked-down-by-
the-wind thing.)

He looks like the type of tall boy
    who would hold the ball over someone else's head

and laugh
if he had the chance.

But he doesn't.
You can see it on his face
    the way his brows constantly furrow
    storm cloud ready to bring down a tempest at any time
    the way he folds his arms
        because he has no reason to reach out his hand
        and torment anyone
        when he already torments himself.

People would say I should feel sorry for him.

(People would say I need to Think Hard about the fact
    that I know the way that face feels on the inside
        how tight your forehead feels
        and your chest
        always
        in the middle of the night
        when you can't ignore it.

As if it is easy to Think Hard on things
that already don't let you forget about them
when you so
very
badly
want to.

As if giving them more attention will make them
shrivel up and die
rather than fueling them
stroking them like a mosquito bite to hot, itchy
annoyance
letting them grow.)

But I don't
And I won't.

Colin Clayborne and his tall, storm-cloud self
isn't the only one with problems.

Twenty

Maria was in a foul mood when she woke up the next morning.

It didn't help that her head was pounding and her stomach clenching like she'd eaten something bad. She groaned as she tried to sit up, then let her head fall down to the bed. Had she worked herself up yelling at Colin yesterday?

That was what Phuppo always said when she draped herself over the couch. "Look at how you worked me up over nothing, Maria. I have a migraine and your uncle's going to be home from work, and I've done nothing today. Nothing but try to talk you down. Now look at me."

(Maria always looked. If anyone had asked her, she would say that Phuppo looked pretty fine lying there with a cold towel over her head, moodily eating the chickpeas out of her spiced snack mix and checking for drama reruns on the TV.)

But Maria wasn't an auntie.

And this felt dreadfully familiar.

A peek under the sheets confirmed her suspicions.

She was on her period.

"Ugh!" Maria hit her head against her pillow again and regretted it as her head throbbed in response.

She'd gotten her period young—like her mom, who was thrilled to "bond" over it, while Maria was grossed out and embarrassed. But then her parents died not long after, and it hadn't been . . . well, there much at all after that.

"It happens," Phuppo's family doctor had said, waving his hand dismissively. "She's been through trauma. The body has its ways of coping. She's young. It'll come back."

Maria had never seen Phuppo so angry.

"How does he know what the body does, when he's never had to deal with this?" she seethed, forcing Maria to drink some bitter concoction and firmly patting her shoulders. "It's fine, beta. We'll find a way to help this."

But of course, whatever she had intended to do, she'd sent Maria on to America without it.

There was a knock at her door. Maria forced herself up on her elbows, heart sinking. It couldn't be Colin, could it?

He was the last person she wanted to talk to. And of course, he would choose *now,* after sulking at the dinner table last night and not saying a word to her, then slouching upstairs with his earbuds to do his homework or saw away at his violin.

The house could feel the tension between them too. She'd felt the floor jiggling, nudging the table so she lurched sideways as Colin reached over her for the butter and giving little encouraging vibrations when Maria slid back her chair to leave.

She wasn't sure why it was so invested in their making up. She didn't care, either. Let the house do what it wanted.

She was going to keep her silence.

Maria was pretty good when it came to vows of silence. Most people itched in those first five minutes —the feeling of not really getting in the last word, or having to warn someone that the stove was still on. But that wasn't when you would slip up.

It would be an hour in, or maybe two. And that would be worse.

Because it wouldn't be itchy. It wouldn't be anything at all. It would just be the easing up of scrunched-together muscles, and the hot blotch of anger flowing out of your cheeks and back down to your fingers and toes, where it would hide until another day.

It would be entirely normal.

And then you would open your silly mouth and move your silly tongue before you could catch either of them.

Adults made this mistake a lot.

Maria didn't care about the itchiness, or filling up the hollow silence afterward. Most people didn't want to talk to Maria—not that she wanted to talk to them either—so it wasn't a problem she particularly worried about.

But it was surprisingly uncomfortable not being on speaking terms with Colin.

Lyndsay cast anxious glances between the two of them, probably wondering why they'd gone back to stony silence after two relatively civil weeks of being able to sit in the same room and not kill each other.

Even Charlotte raised her eyebrows as she lowered her water glass.

If Colin had said something last night—even something quick and mean under his breath—Maria would have been ready to pull him apart.

So of course he would wait to pounce until this morning, when she felt disgusting.

They were too alike. Maria scowled.

She *hated* the thought of it. But everyone said so: Lyndsay, Charlotte with a disapproving sniff, even Mimi.

At least she didn't act all "Woe is me, my life is awful." Like other people didn't have problems.

There was another knock, and Maria froze in place.

"Maria? It's Lyndsay." The familiar tentative voice eased through the cracked door. "It's really late—don't you want breakfast?"

"I can't eat right now." Maria groaned, shifting so she could press her arm over her stomach.

That should have been enough to get Lyndsay to leave. She wasn't the type of adult who thought it meant they had "won" when they pretend-cared you into letting them in. Phuppo was that type, and always shouldered her way through. Never mind a locked door. You didn't lock your phuppo out.

For some reason, the thought of Phuppo barging in to lay hands on her face and go, "What's wrong, beta?" made Maria's eyes water. She tugged her covers over her head.

She hated this.

There was silence for a moment, and then—to Maria's surprise—the door creaked open and Maria heard the sound of feet padding toward her.

"Are you okay?"

"No," Maria grumbled.

The covers tugged away from her, and reluctantly Maria let them go. Lyndsay was leaning over her.

Her dark eyes looked . . . concerned.

Worried.

Worried for *Maria*.

"What's going on? Do you feel hot?" Lyndsay's cool hand darted out and pressed briefly against Maria's forehead, and Maria almost sighed aloud. It made her head throb a little less. "You don't seem to have a fever."

"I just . . . don't feel good."

"Do you need me to call a doctor? You should eat something."

"I can't move from the bed, so don't ask me." Maria shifted onto her stomach and clenched her eyes shut, willing Lyndsay to go away.

There was an awkward silence.

And then, delicately, Lyndsay cleared her throat.

"Maria?" A hand rested on her back. "Hey, it's okay. Do you need me to get you some pads? Did you stain the sheets?"

Maria's face burst into flames. Lyndsay knew. *Lyndsay knew.* It hadn't been embarrassing when Ammu figured out the first time, or when Phuppo passed her some pads with a knowing nod. "Keep those on you, beta, so you aren't caught by surprise."

But for some reason, this was too mortifying for words.

"I don't need anything!" Maria writhed, both in pain and

embarrassment. Ugh, ugh, *ugh.* "Just . . . go away!"

And Lyndsay did.

Of course she got away while the getting was good.

Maria nuzzled her face into her pillow and—when she was sure she had buried herself deep enough—gave a little sniff.

Fine. She could do this alone.

But she missed Ammu.

More than Phuppo's brews or a painkiller or even fresh sheets, she just really, really wanted her mom.

At the sound of a creak, Maria startled upward, not even caring about her messy hair and red face.

Surely the house couldn't make that happen for her—could it?

But it was only Lyndsay, carrying a tray.

"Move over," she said, and when Maria simply blinked at her, she made room for herself, perching on the edge of the bed.

"Pads," she listed, taking them off the tray and plopping them in her lap. "Painkiller—eat that piece of toast and then swallow that. Spare sheets. While you freshen up, I'll throw these in the washer. Do you have another pajama shirt?"

"Why are you here?"

Lyndsay didn't answer, motioning to the other items on the tray. "I know how you feel about my tea blends by now, so I grabbed a few I already had on hand that are good for cramps. Here's a cup of hot water. I was going to make it and bring it up to you, but some of them smell a bit strong. Sniff and see which one your stomach can handle."

She moved toward the cup, but Maria reached out and grabbed her hand.

"Didn't you hear me?"

Lyndsay sighed and looked her full in the face. "I heard you, Maria. I'm here because, whether you or Colin believe it or not, I'm not a boogeyman and I don't like it that you're in pain. I know what it's like to be crampy, and if I can make it better for you, I *want* to make it better."

Maria narrowed her eyes. It was a pretty speech, but with grown-ups, there was always an ulterior motive.

"Don't believe me if you don't want to!" Lyndsay added, raising her hands. "But at least don't believe me and hustle to the bathroom."

Maria grudgingly grabbed the pads and inched herself out of the bed, wincing at the damp spot.

"It's okay," Lyndsay coaxed. "Nothing I haven't seen before. Grab your pajamas and get going. Colin's on an errand with Charlotte, so you don't have to worry about seeing him."

Maria's stomach unknotted. *Thank goodness.*

By the time Maria freshened up—and yes, it did feel

much better—and hobbled back to the bedroom, Lyndsay was turning down fresh sheets.

"Get under," she said.

Maria crawled in, and Lyndsay tucked the blankets around her, giving her a gentle pat.

"There. Okay, tea?"

Maria reached for a small black container. "What's this one?"

"Black cohosh and rosehip. That's the one that smells a little funky, and it does taste a little like iron. But that's good, because it'll build your blood back up."

Maria took a sniff, and her nose wrinkled. "Ugh, not that."

Lyndsay chuckled. "How about raspberry leaf?"

Maria sniffed, and sniffed again. It smelled a little strong, and sharp, like black tea, but nice.

"This one is okay."

Lyndsay dumped the tea bag into the water.

"There we go. I didn't bring any sugar."

"Thank you," Maria said, and meant it. Lyndsay didn't say anything, though a slight smile pulled at her lips.

"Now that you're comfortable, what's the story?"

"Story?" Maria was staring into the depths of the tea, watching as it unfurled from the bag and seeped into the water. The question startled her. Was she supposed to share some sort of story now? Was that how American people dealt with their periods?

"You and Colin were getting along—don't give me that look, at least you were tolerating each other. And now he's . . . well, his usual charming self, and you won't even sit next to him."

Oh. That.

Maria huffed. "Boys are annoying, and he is the most annoying."

She expected Lyndsay to frown and defend Colin. Charlotte definitely would have.

Instead, though, Lyndsay nodded.

"They can be, and it's definitely not right if he did something to upset you and won't apologize for it. Did he?"

"Yes. No. He did something wrong, but he thinks he was right."

Maria wasn't sure why she was sharing. Maybe it was because, like that day in Lowe's, Lyndsay's face was soft and open.

"I just didn't like that he couldn't admit he was wrong," Maria mumbled. "That's it."

She stared down into her tea. Lyndsay was probably going to say she was being too sensitive. Not to take a grumpy boy with a bad attitude to heart.

But the way Colin had said it . . .

"*Why do you care so much about this place? It's not like it's yours!*"

He was right. Wrong about the plants, but right that it wasn't her garden.

It wasn't her home.

Why tie herself up in knots about it when he was right?

Lyndsay studied her, brow furrowed, and then said suddenly, "You know, I wish I could be more like you."

"What?"

That was definitely not what Maria was expecting to hear.

"When you think someone's treated you wrong, you hold them accountable. That's the way it should be." Lyndsay looked off toward the door, her eyes distant. "Sometimes I wonder what my life would have looked like if I hadn't always thought I needed to be nice. I've lost a lot of myself doing that."

She looked back at Maria and smiled, brushing a hand over Maria's head. "You are your own person, Maria, and that's a good thing. Don't forget that."

Maria's mind flashed to Lyndsay's kitchen: how she hid away in it so much, preparing food that Charlotte liked rather than what she seemed to enjoy herself.

Maybe it was more tiresome to be Lyndsay than she had thought.

"Is it too late to do that?" Maria blurted out. When

Lyndsay turned to look at her, she elaborated, face flushing. "To not be nice and do what you want."

Why was she trying, yet again, to make Lyndsay Clayborne feel better?

She wasn't sure, and she could tell Lyndsay wasn't either. But after a moment, the woman smiled.

"Thanks for that, Maria. I'll keep my mind open and see if you're right. Oh, by the way—Mimi called. She invited you over to meet her grandmother. I told her I thought you weren't feeling well."

Mimi and Rick's dadima—their father's stepmother—had been in Dubai visiting her other kids all this time. But if she was back, they could ask her what else to do about the damage from the cold snap. It was an opportunity she couldn't pass up, even if she was in pain.

"I want to go!"

She tried to kick off the covers, and then winced.

"Ow."

Lyndsay patted her leg. "Eat your toast, take a painkiller, and then nap for a bit. It's not even lunchtime yet. I'll take you over in a little while. We can drive so you don't have to walk."

Maria nodded, reaching for her tea. She took a sip, and her eyes widened.

"I like that."

"Oh, thank goodness. A cup of tea you like."

Maria took another sip and murmured, "But I really would like some noon chai."

"Noon chai," Lyndsay repeated absently to herself. "Maybe I should look into that. I wonder if it's anything like any of the teas my ama used to make."

She stood, pushing a stack of books aside. "And I should also get a bookshelf in here for you, it looks like. Oh, and Maria?"

Maria looked up.

Lyndsay smiled at her, hugging the tray to her chest.

"Don't worry too much about Colin. I have a feeling he'll come around."

Maria snorted.

She wasn't going to count on it.

Twenty-One

The tea did soothe Maria's stomach. At least at first.

But the closer the car got to Mimi and Rick's house, the tighter the knots got. When Mimi hauled open the car door with her usual excitement, Maria nearly toppled out.

"Oh my gosh!" Mimi gasped. "Are you okay?"

Lyndsay winced in sympathy, rushing around the car to help Maria.

"I can take you back home if the cramps have started back up."

Maria hated to admit to herself how tempting the offer was. But . . .

"No," she grumbled. "You can go. I'll be fine."

Mimi helped her limp toward the door.

"Is it really that bad?" she asked anxiously.

"Yes. No. I . . ." Maria inhaled. Held it.

"I think I'm just a bit nervous. I don't look nice or anything."

"Don't be that way, you're always cute," Mimi said, and grabbed Maria by the arm. Before Maria could prepare herself, Mimi had swung open the front door.

"Dadima, my friend is here!"

Maria had experience with dadimas, and it always left her a little unnerved.

Her own wasn't bad, from her vague memories. She looked like Maria's baba around the cheeks, had a long, elegant nose, and always laughed, and pinched Maria's cheek, and stuffed sweets in her face "to make you a little less sour."

She was always more of a naanu girl, if she was honest. But if her dadima had still been around to live with, she wouldn't have said no.

Other dadimas had a habit of staring, asking awkward questions she wasn't sure she could answer, and being a reminder of everything she didn't have.

Mimi and Rick's dadima was nothing like that. She rushed from one of the back rooms to greet them.

She had a soft, round face and wore a long white sari—the sign of an old widow used to the traditional color of mourning, regardless of how many years it had been since her husband died.

"Welcome, Maria!" a voice called from the kitchen. It sounded very motherly, so Maria assumed that was who it was. "Make yourself at home, all right? And please don't leave before saying hi to me this time!"

"Uh," Maria said, because she was focused on the dadima. Her stomach churned.

"Well," Dadima said, and reached out to pet Maria's cheek. Maria let her.

You had to let dadimas do such things.

For once, though, it actually felt nice.

"Yes, I can tell you're good with gardens," Dadima said after looking at her for a moment. "You have it on your face."

Maria had never been told such a kind thing in her life. Her cheeks flushed.

"I've heard all about you from my grandchildren," Dadima said. "They say that you have a lot of spirit. I'm so glad you're having fun together."

"I'm glad too," Maria said.

It felt odd, to find the right polite words. But this dadi deserved all the respect she could muster.

"Please sit down," Dadima said, steering her into the kitchen. There, a cheery woman who looked just like an older

Mimi rushed over to kiss her on both cheeks.

"Oh! I didn't get a proper introduction at the milaad, but . . . look at you, shundor! You were already so pretty, and you've just gotten prettier. It must be all that fresh air!"

She did look exactly like someone Maria's ammu would have loved. Maria's heart ached.

"Come, take some shemai," Dadima coaxed, passing her plate. "I know you have gardening questions, and we'll get to that, but it's important to take a breath too."

Maria got a lump in her throat, and nodded to hide it. Who was this woman, and why was she making Maria feel like butter set out to thaw on a warm plate—remembering what it was like to melt and slide apart and relax?

"The cold snap," Maria said shyly. "That's one thing I want to ask about."

"Oh, yes, I know. And we can also talk about what you want to plant. You were right, by the way. Rick told me that you thought it was a vegetable garden, and that's exactly how I remember it. I can tell you what Saira had there. But for now, eat your sweet."

"Thank you," Maria managed. She wasn't sure why she felt so emotional.

And apparently Dadi wasn't done. She leaned in, her eyes narrowed. Maria backed up a little bit. What was happening now?

"Your face . . . ," she said slowly. "You look like a neighbor I had when I used to live in Dubai."

"I have a lot of relatives. I lived in Dubai at one point too."

Dadi's eyes widened. "Really? We'll have to talk about that. Hmm, I wish I could remember the name of the woman. It started with an A . . . Ambreen, I think. Ambreen Dhar."

Maria's eyes widened.

"Phuppo? You know my phuppo?"

"Oh, so she's your father's sister?"

"Yes, she is!"

"What a small world it is." Dadi chuckled. "My son worked with her husband. So you must be the niece, then, that stayed with them from time to time when her parents were away. She always seemed excited that she would get to see you, and I heard that was why they moved back to Lahore—so that they could have a home for you to come to."

Maria's mind was reeling. The very thought of Phuppo accommodating her that much when she was always sighing her way through a migraine when Maria was around was . . . wild.

"Actually . . ." Dadi stood up, groaning a little, and motioned for Maria to follow. "Come here a moment."

Maria followed her down a hallway into a small, pleasant room. The windows were open so that sunlight streamed in. A prayer rug was spread across the floor, with the corner carefully folded over in the same way that all South Asian grandmas seemed to leave their janamaz, along with the same cold cream her naanu used on a nightstand, and a little plant angled on the dresser to get enough light.

Dadi rummaged through her nightstand drawer, emerging triumphantly with a phone book.

"Now, it's been a few years, but . . . ah, here it is. Ambreen Dhar's cell-phone number."

She extended the page to Maria. Maria stared down at it.

"Have you talked to her since you got here?"

"No, but . . ." The words burst out of Maria like water from a broken pipe. "She sent me away. I mean, the student association my parents were part of in college—their old friends . . . they said it was better for me here, like I was suffering there, but they didn't even ask if that was what I wanted. But Phuppo didn't stand up to them. I'm not sure she cares at all."

"Home often misses you as much as you miss home," Dadima said. "And it's not easy to send off a child that's your own family."

She squeezed Maria's shoulder gently. "I think I have a calling card. Wait a moment."

Dadima fumbled in her purse. Maria watched her

anxiously. Why was she getting swept up into this woman's whims?

"Here." Dadima handed it to her, along with the phone number. "You don't have to decide if you want to talk to her right now. But it's always good to have the option, right?"

Maria nodded, staring down at the number.

Why was her heart pounding at the thought of hearing her aunt's voice?

She drifted dazedly behind Dadima back to the kitchen, where Mimi's mom rested a tender hand on her shoulder to ask if she wanted Rooh Afza in water or milk.

(Of course she wanted it in milk.

She didn't have bad taste.

But she didn't say it that way.)

After that, Mimi's mom brought out more sweets, and it turned out that Mimi and Rick remembered how to play ludo with her.

And it was wonderful.

Peaceful.

Maria forgot about the ache in her stomach and her head. She forgot about Colin too.

At least until the doorbell rang.

"I'll get it," Mimi called, and rushed forward. The door swung open.

The boy standing there had his head bowed. He was mumbling something under his breath—as though he was practicing to get it just right.

He raised his head, and his eyes met Maria's.

"Colin," Maria whispered.

Twenty-Two

All the happiness Maria was feeling sank down to her toes.

What was Colin doing here?

She turned around, expecting Mimi and Rick to be just as shocked. But neither of them seemed surprised at all.

"Oh, good, Colin's here," Rick said. "Let me go and get my plant books."

He got up off the floor, Noodles cupped in his hands, and disappeared into his room.

Mimi just beamed from ear to ear, and her mom was already rushing to the door, hands clasped to her chest as though she was seeing a long-lost relative.

"Colin, how are you, sweetheart? It's been such a long time. You probably don't remember me, but I used to hold you when you were a baby . . . oh, you've gotten so tall!"

"Nice to meet you, Ms. Rehman," Colin said, but his eyes were fixed on Maria.

Maria folded her arms over her chest, scowling back.

A hand reached out and gently pushed her arms down.

"What . . ."

She turned to look into the kind brown eyes of Dadima.

"Don't be like that, ma," Dadima gently chided. That was the way Bangladeshi family members always referred lovingly to children they knew: ma, or ammu, or baba, even though there was no way they were these old ladies' parents. It might have been weird to someone else, but it made Maria's heart warm.

"Like what?" Maria could hear the sharpness in her voice, and for the first time, it made her cringe.

But Dadima just smiled, lifting her hand to clutch Maria's chin affectionately. She shook it slightly, and the familiar movement made Maria's eyes sting.

It was such a grandmother thing to do, and no one had done it since her own, many years ago when her grandmother still had all her memories and more patience than anyone else to deal with Maria's tantrums and huffing and pouts.

"You and that boy had a fight, right?"

Maria looked down. There was no use denying it. "Yes. Well, kind of. We're not friends or anything, to really have a fight."

"Hmm." Dadima hummed at that. "And whose fault was it?"

Maria bristled. "His! Just ask Rick and Mimi. He made us put in the plants, and then they died."

"But did he mean for the plants to die?"

Maria wanted to say yes. Of course he had, with those annoying earbuds always plugged in and his shoulders hunched over like he was trying to tune them out, like . . .

Like she did when the noise got too much for her.

"No," she grudgingly forced out. "I don't think he did."

"And he didn't hurt you, during this fight?" Dadima asked. "Because if he did, I can have Rick throw him out."

She pantomimed Colin tumbling through the door, head over heels.

Maria narrowed her eyes at Rick. He looked both too scrawny and too excited to show Colin his plant books to be reliable.

So, as tempting as that sounded . . .

"No," Maria mumbled. "He just made me mad."

"It happens," Dadima said mildly. "At least hear him out. Then decide what you want to do with him. If he doesn't apologize—well, that's another thing. I don't think girls should have any time for boys who can't admit when they're wrong."

Dadima stepped toward Colin, who was listening to Rick read something from one of the plant books. Maria stayed right where she was, fidgeting with her fingers.

"Hello there, Colin," Dadima said.

Colin's response was too low for Maria to hear. She inched forward a little bit—not enough to act like she cared what was happening.

No. Not at all.

Enough to hear in case it got interesting.

Dadi had a hand on Colin's shoulder and a wide smile on her face. Colin looked uncomfortable, as though he was unsure what to do with himself and all the people reaching out and asking him how he was. The way she had looked when she first stepped into the house.

Maria's heart ached.

She rubbed her chest, annoyed.

Maybe those horrible cramps migrated around your body. That had to be it.

Whatever. She had dealt with it, and she'd found that they were all nice people. Colin could too. She didn't have to go over there and rescue him.

"... your mom," Dadima was saying. "I'm sure she would

have been proud that you're gardening. I used to go over and help her sometimes, and she would have you at her feet in a little bouncing chair."

She chuckled at the memory.

"She would pick you right up with dirt under her fingers, and show you everything. She was so happy to have you there with her."

Colin swallowed hard. To Maria's horror, he looked like he was going to cry.

"That's . . . uh. No one's ever told me that. Thanks."

Dadima reached out and patted his cheek. "Let me get you some fruit."

As she wandered off to the kitchen, Mimi's mom circled back, still smiling widely.

"It's so nice to see you back here," Mimi's mother chimed. "It's been awhile. We always meant to stay in touch, but . . . well, it's hard when you haven't spoken to someone, and we haven't seen your father in a while."

Colin squirmed, his cheeks flushing.

"He seems to be away a lot," Ms. Rehman continued. Colin hunched his shoulders in response.

Maria drew herself up in indignation. Yes, she knew that Desi people loved to gossip, and that fishing for information about your parents and family life was as commonplace as breathing air—but how could Mimi's mom not notice his discomfort?

"Colin!"

There was a scuffling noise, and everyone stared. It took her a moment to realize why: she had popped right in between Mimi's mom and Colin.

Colin gaped at her.

"Colin!" Maria barked again.

"Y-yes!"

"You came because you had something to say to me, right? So come on and say it. Right now. Outside. Let's get it over with."

"What?" Colin glanced wildly at Dadima, who came back from the kitchen holding a plate of watermelon slices like nothing was happening.

"That sounds like a good idea," Dadima said cheerily. "Go on, talk to each other and come back for some fruit. You're hungry, right, Colin? Of course you are."

"I have some biryani in the kitchen," Mimi's mom said, as though Maria hadn't interrupted them. When Maria looked at her in amazement, she *winked*.

"Go out and have a good talk."

Colin looked flustered. "I . . ."

But Colin didn't get to finish his sentence, because Maria

marched over and grabbed him by the forearm. She tugged him forward, fuming.

He didn't take a hint at all. And here she was, making a scene to rescue him.

"We'll be outside for a minute," she told the very unsurprised-looking adults.

"Take your time." Ms. Rehman smiled.

Rick and Mimi didn't turn around from where they were busily helping Dadima cut up fruit, but there was something about their shoulders that made Maria sure they were . . . happy about something.

Not just happy. Triumphant.

Maria had a suspicion that she had been set up—but in what way, and for what reason, she wasn't entirely sure. She didn't want to inspect it too deeply.

Why did she get like this over Colin? She . . . forgot how to be herself—the Maria who didn't get involved in other people's sob stories, and focused on entering and leaving the room with as little attention as possible.

Was this what happened when she spent too much time around nice grandmas? If that was the case, she needed to be more careful in the future.

Colin cleared his throat.

"Hey, Maria."

Maria made it clear that she was glaring at the slats that made up the porch, and not paying attention to how close he was coming.

He came closer, and closer, and then stopped.

"What?" Maria barked without looking at him.

"What do you mean, what . . ." Colin exhaled, and shook his head. "No. I'm sorry. Let's not start fighting again. I liked it better when we were peaceful."

Maria looked at him out of the corner of her eye. "Really?"

"Yeah. I wanted to say that this morning, but well . . . you didn't come down to breakfast. Look, you were right, okay? I should have been paying attention to the weather, and not put everything on Rick only to blame him afterward. It doesn't matter that it's my mom's garden. I don't know anything, and it was worse because . . ."

Colin leaned against the porch railing with a sigh. "I . . . well, I made it seem like I was suspended. The school let me make the call to Dad, and it doesn't seem like either he or Lyndsay really needed to hear more than, 'Colin messed up again.' I honestly think if Dad knew the whole story, he would have stepped in and made sure I stayed there. But I wanted to come home from the conservatory because I need to think. I was having a hard time studying and focusing. And then my counselor had this talk with me."

Maria waited, arms folded.

"Look. Have you ever just . . . felt totally overwhelmed? Like you don't know where to start, so you just let things go? And sometimes, every single noise makes you want to scream?"

Maria was surprised. That sounded like her a lot of the time.

Most days.

"Maybe," she said. "Doesn't everyone?"

"I thought so, but my counselor says that it actually might be something like ADHD." Colin delivered this with the same solemness someone else might say, "She told me I'm dying."

Maria turned that over in her head. ADHD. Could that explain how she felt too—wanting things to be quiet, but not too quiet, always fidgeting and getting irritated people were in her space? It was a relief to have a name to put to it, to look it up later and see if there was more familiarity in it than what Colin was describing, but he was acting like it was a bad thing. "That's it?"

"That's *it*?" Colin's eyes widened. "You know how my grandma would react hearing about that? No Clayborne has ever had a learning disorder, or ADHD, or anything like that. And then my counselor said she wanted to talk to my dad!

There's no way I could talk to him about that. He would just . . . it's not what Claybornes *do*."

"I'm not sure why you care so much about what your grandma and dad think. Isn't it *your* brain?" Maria demanded. "Why do you care about what they think when it's hurting you and they don't even notice?"

Colin stared hard at her.

"Maria . . . are you angry at them for me?"

"No," Maria said. "I'm amazed at how ridiculous you're being over your grandma when she spends most of her life in a pink robe eating gross soups."

"Thank you."

Maria didn't expect that.

"What?"

"Thank you. And . . . I'm sorry. For before."

"Whatever." Maria sniffed. This conversation was getting too gooey for her tastes.

"No, really." Colin paused, and then, looking shy, said, "I mean it when I say thank you. You're the reason I'm in my mom's garden again. Because of you, I feel more . . . connected."

Maria's cheeks warmed. Connected?

Colin looked down.

"That was what the Desi kids at school used to say when Dad still made an effort. When we used to go to the parties and celebrations and stuff like that. Either you're connected, or you're not. You're Desi enough, or not."

Oh.

Maria recognized that thin, helpless look on Colin's face.

She understood what he meant, even if she didn't want to admit it directly to him—that lack of connection and community even if you were surrounded by it. She pictured Colin, thin shouldered and kurta clad, scrunched in between uncaring uncles and suspicious-eyed boys.

His father would be there, of course. But did that help at all?

Maria didn't realize she had said it aloud until Colin shook his head.

"He would just tell me to toughen up."

At the look of surprise on Maria's face, his darkened.

"My dad isn't . . . well, you'll see. Eventually."

Something about Colin's expression kept her from asking more.

He looked away, and Maria swallowed. She had a feeling she was about to say something that would hurt her pride, but somehow that look on Colin's face hurt her even more.

"Colin . . . I don't like anyone."

Well, that wasn't what she had meant to say, but at least it wiped that look off Colin's face. The amusement wasn't any better, though.

"Really?"

"I don't!" Maria almost stamped her foot. "I really, really don't."

"You spend a lot of time cuddling with Lyndsay."

Maria gaped at him, her cheeks flushing.

"I do *not*."

"She lets you into her kitchen. She doesn't even let Grandma into her kitchen."

"Your grandma is a witch."

"She is," Colin agreed. "And not even the cool kind."

Maria waved him off. "Anyway, I don't know what you're talking about. I don't like anyone. I don't like Lyndsay. I don't like Mimi, and I don't like Rick. And I really don't like you."

"Which is why you dragged me out here so I didn't have to talk about my problems in front of them," Colin interrupted.

Maria glowered at him. His eyes were a little too bright, a little too . . . happy.

Trusting.

Those were things no one should have in their eyes, looking at her.

"But . . . ," she started, and then paused.

"But?" Colin leaned in.

"I don't like any of you for different reasons. And your

being Desi, or not Desi, has nothing to do with it."

Her entire face felt like she'd lit a match and then held it on her tongue. Steam had to be billowing out of her ears. Maria focused on Colin's forehead. It seemed like the safest place on him to look right now.

Colin smiled, and he reached out to her shoulders, which had bunched up. He gently pushed them down. "All right. Don't hurt yourself."

Maria stayed tense, waiting for him to move back.

But he just stood there.

"Have you heard of personal space?" she snapped.

"I have. Just . . ."

Suddenly, his arms were around her. She went stiff, for one moment, and then she was hugging him back.

It was honestly a moment of weakness.

Maria didn't usually have them.

But then, she hadn't known Colin before.

Maria shook him off.

"Okay. Gross. Let's get back to work."

Colin laughed. But it died away when he saw her expression.

"Wait, right now? Can't we have fruit first?"

"Did you all make up?" Rick chimed in cheerfully. He and Mimi were leaning out the screen door, plates in hands and very smug expressions on their faces. "That's great. Come on, let's go and talk to Dadima about the plants."

Maria glared at them, but it was not effective. Rick tugged Colin off the porch, and Colin went with him.

Mimi sidled up to Maria.

"Feel better?"

"You're too nosy," Maria grumbled.

But she did feel better.

Her heart felt full, with Colin and Rick chattering in front of her and Mimi humming at her side.

Everything was coming together.

XII ✦ *First Bloom*

I

Blooming is quite ugly.
Shocking, after all this expectation,
to see green skin split
yielding to pulpy, yellow mess.
But all things grow into beauty.

II

Maria prefers
the unfinished bloom that clings
seeking her kind warmth
reminding her all too much
of herself, plucked from afar.

III

She has never felt
like the brightest bloom in sight
or a bloom at all.
Prickly, ugly, messy girl.
But when Colin smiles, she brightens.

IV
Her heart feels fuller
brighter, warmer, roomier than before
knowing that she has
brought out that tentative look.
Elusive, hopeful flower.

Twenty-Three

Dadima was an amazing resource.

And she didn't ask the questions Maria feared, like "Exactly where is this little patch of earth?" or "Why are you all asking about plots and squares and wide spaces if you've been given such a tiny corner?" or the most nightmarish of all, "Does Lyndsay know what you all are doing out there, Maria?"

She did ask questions that Maria hadn't thought of: "Did you test the soil for moistness with your finger?" and "Did you consider where your shade plants should be?" and "Did you know laau needs some proper lattice to work its way up so its blossoms can get enough sun?"

"I told you she would help," Mimi said smugly as Dadima

held up a finger and walked into the spare room that was apparently her makeshift greenhouse.

"Does she do this professionally or something?"

Mimi beamed from ear to ear.

"She taught herself. Look!"

Dadima came back to the living room, arms full of potted plants.

"These are what you need," she huffed, putting them down on the glass coffee table and ignoring Ms. Rehman's distant wail of, "Ma, my coffee table!"

"As you all learned the hard way, the weather needs to be considered as much as the state of the ground. We've passed the last of the frost, so you should be able to start planting safely now—but slowly. You don't want to rush when putting anything in the earth. Focus on tilling it and tending to it. Be patient and make sure that it's ready for plants."

Maria leaned forward in spite of herself, but it was Colin who spoke.

"How do we do that?"

"Feed the ground the way you feed yourself," Dadima said, smiling gently. "Fertilizer. Some extra mulch. Turn up the earth and put your fingers in it. Plan your patches for shade and for sun. And as you plant, keep weeding around them and make sure you're tending to them in the right way. The books I'll give you will help. And you can put these ones"—she gestured to the potted plants on one side of the table—"right into the ground after you've taken care of it. I gave you squash and more kale, because that was the right idea. They should be hearty enough to get you started. And then you can move on to the plants you like."

Maria could feel her face fall.

More weeding and turning up the earth? She was hoping that Dadima would usher them straight to the planting.

"I know that's hard to hear, baby," Dadima said, and Maria's head reared up, surprised that she could be read that easily. Dadima grinned at her. "But remember, plants spread their roots once they find the right patch of earth to welcome them. Flowers open their petals when they have enough energy and light to encourage them to. You will have the garden you want, but you have to prepare for it."

Then Dadima gave them some gardening manuals she liked, and escorted them to Mimi's dad's computer room so they could watch her favorite YouTubers.

Being around Dadima was filling Maria with hope again. The cold snap was a setback, but now . . . now they knew how to combat it.

And that was how they found themselves back outside the next afternoon after the others finished school and Maria logged out of the online program Lyndsay insisted she stay on top of. Armed with hoes and rakes, they broke up the earth. Rick and Noodles crawled around, plucking out stray weed roots, twigs, and fragments of brick and stone.

Colin hung back uncertainly. For a moment Maria was about to snap at him—were they really going to do this again?—but the thought of how open he had been yesterday, how he had said they were partners, made her hold back.

When had she become a softy?

She sighed and walked up to him.

"Hey."

Colin jumped.

"Um . . . what?"

She held out a pair of polka-dotted gardening gloves. "Put on your earbuds if you want and pull weeds. You can do that, can't you?"

Colin looked from the gloves to her face.

And then he gave that wide, shy smile.

"Okay. Yeah . . . uh, thanks."

It was getting very close to sappy fast. Maria rolled her eyes.

"Just do it. We need to get started."

"Okay, okay. Don't bite my head off."

He was still smiling as he took the gloves and Maria turned

away—to see Mimi and Rick grinning in creepily identical ways, and Rick giving her a thumbs-up.

"Do you think the garden is going to till itself?" she snapped. "Come on, back to work."

It definitely wasn't the work she had thought they would be doing. And it didn't go as quickly as she hoped it would.

Every time she got the hang of things, something else sprouted up that she needed to figure out. One day, back aching after an hour of being hunched over, she was yanking up what looked like a totally dead plant when Rick hollered for her to stop.

"Wait, wait, wait! Leave that one in!"

Maria glowered at him. "What? It's dead."

"I don't think so. Look."

Rick squatted next to her, smiling in greeting to the tik-tiki, which had tumbled off Maria's knee, and gently snapped off one branch.

"Well, if it wasn't dead, it's probably dead now," she grumbled.

"Oh, come on, it'll be fine. But look."

Rick held up the branch. Inside, she could see light green.

"It's alive," she breathed.

"Yep. One of Dadima's friends has a kid who studied at Oxford and calls it wick. It means that the plant is still working on the inside, even if it looks like it's dead on the outside."

"Like the garden," Maria whispered, and earned a wide, freckled smile.

"Exactly."

"Rick!" Mimi cupped her hands around her mouth, even though the garden wasn't *that* big, really. "Ma texted! Dinner's ready!"

"Oh, shoot!" Rick scrambled to his feet. "Coming!"

Maria stayed squatting, staring at the plant still cupped between her hands. It was dawning on her that she had a problem, a big one.

She was frozen in place. Everything hurt.

Was this supposed to happen at her age?

"Maria?" She craned her neck slightly to see Colin above her. At least he wasn't looking as amused as she expected.

Mostly.

"Um, will you bite off my head if I offer you a hand?"

Ugh. Maria sighed. "No."

Colin helped her up, and they pulled the gate closed behind them after he collected his violin case. As the weather had gotten nicer, he seemed to bring it outside more often. Maria was apprehensive at first, considering the grim dirges he seemed fond of playing, but it was surprisingly enjoyable background noise while gardening.

Now, as they walked, she pointed at the case.

"Has your grandma asked about your practicing, and why you do it outside?"

Colin shrugged. "I guess she's just happy I'm doing it at all. I'm glad she isn't hovering, honestly. I can get my homework done without her weighing in on what pieces would be 'ambitious' enough, and it's less stressful. I want to try this new one, *Flight of the Bumblebee. It's difficult, but I* think I can do it."

Maria nodded encouragingly.

She liked the name of the piece. It reminded her of the garden—fresh and lively.

They walked through the back hallway, Maria shucking off her shoes. After a moment's pause, Colin did too.

"It feels better," he said to her raised eyebrows.

When they stepped into the kitchen, Lyndsay was excitedly talking into her phone.

"I know, yes . . . oh, Maria!" she gushed, rushing toward her. Maria's eyes widened. That didn't sound good. "Asra, Maria's here. Maria, say hi—Asra managed to FaceTime today!"

The name made Maria's blood run cold.

Asra? FaceTiming instead of a phone call?

This wasn't good at all.

Lyndsay turned the phone, and Maria was faced with a

vaguely familiar face on the screen—only a little bigger than she expected it to be.

"Oh, oh, wait," a voice said from the other end, and then Asra was there, beaming embarrassedly. "I always forget how large this camera makes everything, I . . ."

She stopped and stared.

"But . . . is . . ."

Her face loomed large again as she moved closer to the screen.

"Is that really Maria?"

Lyndsay giggled. "Last I checked!"

"Salaam," Maria managed. Lyndsay had never insisted on her speaking to Asra before. The thoughts of why she would be expected to now had her stomach in knots.

"Goodness, you look so . . ." Asra paused and then started again. "Like you've been getting sun! That's good. It's . . . I'm so glad to see it."

"Thank you," Maria mumbled.

Lyndsay took the phone back. "I'd be surprised if she didn't look like she was getting some fresh air. She and Colin have been spending a lot of time outside. They like to garden with the kids down the street."

"Outdoors? Helping? Maria?" Asra sounded faint. "Wow. A lot is happening. But is everything really okay, Lyndsay?

She's . . . not putting you through any trouble?"

"Who, Maria?" Lyndsay glanced at Maria. "No, she's lovely. I've got her doing some online classes, and I've made plans for fall enrollment if it comes down to it. Don't worry about staying there longer. We've got everything under control."

A little warmth glowed in Maria's chest at those words. *She's lovely.*

Colin nudged Maria. "Now's our time to escape. Come on."

They climbed the stairs, Colin saying something about being grateful that he wasn't roped in to say hi to some random lady.

Maria could hardly hear him.

Why had she reacted so strongly to Asra's call?

Had she forgotten, just a little bit, that all this was temporary?

Pretending she could stay here? That Lyndsay cared about her?

"Maria?" A hand cupped her elbow. Colin looked down at her in concern. "You okay?"

She wasn't.

She was as far as possible from okay.

But the thing about being Maria Latif . . . was that she never showed it.

"I'm fine," she said, nodding firmly. "Just thinking about what else we need to do tomorrow."

Colin's forehead smoothed.

"The back corner, right? I was thinking . . ."

Maria followed him into his room and took a seat on the floor, giving acidic responses in all the right places.

It would be okay. It had to be.

XIII ❧ What Makes a Home

Home is

where you take your dupatta off
    (or orna
    depending on which family is near
    which culture feels closer for the day
    or the season or the mood)

and fling it
    dramatically
    Bollywood-beauty style
    to whichever chair or sofa it pleases to drape upon.

(Never mind Ammu's rolled eyes
Baba's indulgent shake of his head

because
this is home.)

Home is

where your buckled, heeled, hoof-solid shoes
are eased off
    find their place
    where you fit in your family
    (Baby Bear, at the very end
    just
    right)
    exactly where they need to be.

(And regardless which guests flood in
and how cluttered the foyer becomes
with shucked sandals and worn loafers
your shoes will never be removed from their shelf

because

this is home.)

Home is

where you don't have to coat your tongue in the cloying
honey of
    honorifics
        (auntie grandmother big sister
        layer upon layer crystalizing and being scraped off
        and slapped into conversations as though they are a
warm cup of tea.)

Where you can languish and make large, lazy snow angels
in your parents' pet names for you.
Don't ask permission to eat the last piece of chocolate.

Be
yourself.

Be
at peace.

Be
at home.

This isn't home.

But sometimes when Colin looks Maria's way and
 he doesn't quite
 smile
 but his lips do something at the corners

 a soft calm in his eyes
 a recognition that she is part of his world
 not a threat to it.

Sometimes when Lyndsay absently holds out a spoon
urges with her chin and hand to
sip
taste.
 (Tell me what you think.
 I trust what you think.
 It matters what you think.)

And when the house itself
 feels like it is
 patting Maria on the back as she passes an open door
  tucking her in with wafts of familiar spices
and snatches of old lullabies

embracing her
recognizing her

it feels dangerously
wonderfully

close.

Twenty-Four

It was impractical to assign a feeling to a day.

And when Maria decided this, she wasn't thinking about *her* feelings—which, she would readily admit, tended toward three settings: slightly overcast, stormy, and Bad Weather Alert.

She meant general feelings—the way people get up and decide, "Today is a good day," or "Today is a bad day," without so much as inching out a toe from their bed or turning on the news and letting the world tell them whether or not it actually was good, or bad, or somewhere in between.

But this day, this morning, made her want to break her own rule.

Because it felt good.

Looking out the window and seeing the sunshine soaking into the green lawn—that clear, crisp gold that you only got on the balmiest spring days or autumn afternoons—was good.

Smelling the heady aroma of simmering tomato sauce and spices was good.

She careened down the stairs, two at a time—loving the dangerous, warning glide her socks gave against the smooth wood—and nearly collided with Colin's back.

"Watch it," he griped, but it didn't have the usual peppery bite. It couldn't, with that slight hint of a grin crossing his face as their eyes met.

She knew she had that same, ridiculous look on too.

It was the smile you gave when you shared a secret.

A good secret—the secret that was the most good thing of what she was already (incredibly) deeming a good day.

The plants were blooming.

The garden was returning.

They *were the reason the garden was returning.*

How could it not be a good day?

Lyndsay was humming as they entered the kitchen, and she turned with a bright look of her own.

"Gosh, it hasn't been this temperature in ages," she exclaimed, sliding on polka-dot-patterned mitts to grasp the iron skillet on the stove. Colin danced forward on tiptoe, craning to see what was in the skillet.

"That smells so good," he said dreamily.

Maria rolled her eyes. She was *not* going to act that way over something Lyndsay cooked . . . even if he was right.

"Shakshuka," Lyndsay said grandly, lifting the lid off the skillet. Steam rose from the pan, revealing neat little poached eggs in the midst of lava-red tomato sauce and bright green peppers.

Maria's stomach growled.

Colin was already sliding forward, spooning out an egg and so much sauce it nearly spilled off his plate. He dragged his spoon through, taking a taste. His eyes fluttered closed.

"I love shakshuka," he said.

Lyndsay smiled, a wide, real smile, and ran her fingers through her hair.

Amid straight strands of black, a little glimmer caught the light, like the slightest change of color within the very heart of an open flame: bright, fiery orange.

Mehndi orange, to be specific.

Maria still wasn't sure how that happened. Maybe it was the Rehmans. Mimi and Rick's family energy got to you— made you want to try something to see them smile.

Last night, Lyndsay had arrived to collect her and Colin

from "hanging out"—which could mean lolling around, researching plants, watching movies that Mimi and Rick insisted Maria and Colin were "missing out on," with a sporadic appearance by Mimi and Rick's dad, who spent most of his time in his office but would emerge, blinking owlishly and patting each child kindly on the head if he heard the theme music of an old favorite.

Maria found herself liking their father—which was very unusual to say about an adult. Maybe it was because he felt like Colin, if Colin had a healthier relationship with Lyndsay and Mr. Clayborne, and grew up to have big glasses and rumpled hair and always seem to be reaching for a pencil behind his ear to scribble down a new idea.

Colin too seemed to relax when they were over at Mimi and Rick's house. They even occasionally coaxed him into playing the violin.

Maria could hear his talent and his love for his music as he played. Even if his father and grandmother had made him choose that path, he made it his own, especially now that he chose what he wanted to play.

Usually it made her tense inside, like he was moving in a direction she could never follow. There was no home to ground her, no parents and grandparents coaxing her toward a gift she couldn't seem to find within herself beneath all the tangles of anger and hurt and grief.

But that evening, leaning up against the Rehman sofa and watching as he picked up his bow and nestled his violin under his chin, she felt peaceful.

Even though Mimi was determined to do Maria's hands with mehndi.

"Maria! Stop squirming. Gosh, how are you going to take sewing lessons from me if you can't sit still for this?"

"I don't like getting mehndi done," Maria grumbled as Mimi smacked her wrist—yet again—and drew it back toward her. "Aren't you finished yet?"

"Don't rush me."

Mimi's tongue poked out as she concentrated on making flower petals bloom from the center of Maria's palm.

"You'll love it when it's dry. I promise."

It was the waiting that was the problem. She couldn't do anything until the mehndi was dry enough to not smear everywhere. And it made her palms itch.

"What are you doing?"

Lyndsay's curious voice fell over Maria's head a moment before her hand landed there. Lyndsay was doing that a lot recently: not the quick, furtive shoulder clasps from when Maria first arrived, or the tighter ones dedicated to steering her.

Lingering, gentle touches. Sometimes, when Maria looked up, Lyndsay didn't even seem to realize she was doing it.

It made Maria feel oddly warm inside.

"Oh, this is mehndi—you know, henna?" Mimi said, dimpling as she always did when an adult gave her attention.

(Of course, she did it to everyone, but Maria could be petty about Mimi in her head if she had to suffer like this.)

"It's beautiful," Lyndsay breathed. "You're very good at it, Mimi."

"Oh, thank you! Ammu's the real expert, but I practice a lot."

Dadima shuffled in, reaching out to clasp Lyndsay's arm.

"Lyndsay, how about you sit down? I'll do your mehndi for you. Come now."

Lyndsay raised her hands, backing away. "Oh, no. I cook too much for it to stay on. It'll just wash off when I wash my hands."

Dadima laughed. "It does for us too. Washing before prayers and cooking . . . it will always go away eventually. But shouldn't you enjoy it while it lasts?"

"She tells me that all the time, Lyndsay," Mimi's mom called from the kitchen. She walked in, hands dripping and face as warm and wreathed in smiles as always.

"I always worry about my mehndi coming off too

quickly, or missing the things the kids do when I'm away for work. But that's what makes these things more precious— right, Ma?"

"Exactly." Dadima nodded at her daughter-in-law and turned back to Lyndsay. "If you won't do your hands, how about your hair? I think it would look so lovely on you."

"Hair?" Lyndsay reached up to touch hers reflexively. "Doesn't it make it orange?"

"It can, but your hair is so dark, it will only add some richness, you know?"

Dadima reached out and stroked Lyndsay's hair. Lyndsay let her, eyes soft. Maria could understand.

There was something about Dadima that made you not mind, even if you usually did.

"You really think so?" Lyndsay asked.

Dadima nodded, and Mimi's mom chimed in. "Just give it a try! It's temporary, after all."

Lyndsay looked between the two of them, and then— surprisingly—she turned to Maria, a shy smile on her face.

"What do you think, Maria? Should I try it?"

Maria blinked up at her. Lyndsay was looking at her like her opinion mattered—like she wanted Maria to approve it too.

It wasn't like this was a recipe, or tea.

Maria rolled her eyes. "If you want to suffer too, go right ahead."

She expected Lyndsay to shrink back, the way she would have before. Maybe give an excuse about Charlotte waiting for them, or her husband calling soon. But instead she straightened her shoulders and plopped right down next to Maria.

"Okay. Let's do this."

Maria's eyes widened. Mimi's mom let out a laugh.

"Let's do this!" she echoed.

And they did.

The look on Charlotte's face when Lyndsay walked through the door was priceless.

"What in the world did you *do*?"

"Just a little henna," Lyndsay said, flipping her hair over her shoulder. "Do you like it?"

It was quite obvious Charlotte did not.

But, in the face of Lyndsay's peaceful expression and Tupperware containers chock-full of Dadi's curried eggs, fried rice, and more than a few different types of pickles, it didn't seem like she could muster up the words to say it.

She had taken herself off to "see a gallery exhibition with some information about the Claybornes" very quickly the next morning.

Lyndsay didn't seem to let it bother her.

Things were changing.

Now Maria reached for the toast piled high in the center of the table. She ripped off the grainy crust and sopped it through bright tomato sauce and runny egg, warmed from the inside out. Underneath her feet, the floorboards crackled and hummed reassuringly.

The house was in the same good mood she was.

Colin was already on his second plate, peering down at a piece of paper unfolded across the table.

"Mimi totally traced this," he muttered softly, just so Maria could hear.

Maria snorted, but she understood exactly who—and what—he meant. He was looking at the blueprint of the garden. She wasn't sure why the garden needed a blueprint *now*, when they'd already started unpotting plants and putting them in rows, but Rick insisted on it.

"We're putting down the roots now," Rick said firmly, "but we need to make sure we're planning for how far they spread."

"That's deep," Colin said, sounding grudgingly impressed.

"That's what Dadima told him," Mimi said with a roll of her eyes. "So, who is doing this?"

Rick looked at Maria, who startled back. "Why me?"

"You seem to have a good idea of where everything should go."

Maria glanced at Colin and Mimi. Surely one of them would disagree. She could tell she was too bossy when it came to the garden. Most times, Mimi just scoffed and did it the way she wanted to when Maria was being too much.

But Colin, being Colin, was always good for a fight.

Amazingly, though, he was nodding.

"You do," he said, and Mimi smiled in agreement.

"Come on, Maria. Give it a try."

What else could Maria say to that?

Well, a lot of rude things pointing out how none of them had seen her (nonexistent) artistic talent, or how they were all trying to put their ideas off on her shoulders.

But she didn't say that. She tried to sketch out the garden one evening as she sat at the counter and pretended to nod or shake her head in response to Lyndsay's pointed questions about tea blends and spices. Like she knew anything about any of that.

You gave her good tea, and she drank it.

Lyndsay didn't seem to notice that Maria wasn't paying attention, and from the happy sounds she was making, apparently her cooking experiment was turning out the way she wanted it to.

And Maria finished the blueprint.

But later the reception was . . .

"It's nice," Mimi said kindly.

Maria scowled at her. "Nice" was a word people threw out there when they didn't know what else to tell you.

Rick leaned his head to one side. "Is that a cat?"

"It's the *bench*," Maria snapped, yanking the paper back. "And you're smiling, so you knew that."

"I wasn't smiling!"

Maria glowered at him, watching the corners of his mouth twitch. Noodles was, as always, poking his head out of Rick's shirtfront. Now he leaned curiously toward her paper. She pulled it farther away.

"Don't even think of nibbling on this."

"No, really, Maria," Mimi was saying, eyes still squinted as though she was trying to work out a math problem. "I think it's good. It's just what we need."

"This was a bad idea," Colin mumbled. Maria glowered at him too.

"Why not let Mimi do one?" Rick said mildly, unflappable as always. "She's good at stuff like that. She can base it on yours, Maria."

"All right, fine," Maria said.

They'd see if perfect Mimi did any better than Maria.

The next day, Mimi rubbed her cheek shyly as Maria stared down at the immaculate lines, delicately feathered tree branches, and little gently labeled patches—FLOWER BED, SHADE PLANT BED, COLIN'S MA'S BENCH.

"It's not that good, I know," Mimi said.

"I hate you," Maria said very seriously. "You're such a liar."

"What?" Mimi blinked at her. "Wait . . . does that think you mean it's good?"

Rick laughed. "Better watch out, Maria. She's starting to understand what you mean when you say things like that."

Maria flushed.

Mimi was beaming from ear to ear. "Really? You like it, Maria?"

"Shut up," Maria muttered, shoving the map away. "It's okay. It's . . . *nice*."

That definitely stung coming out, and Colin and Rick's snickers as Mimi's grin grew wider did too.

But it also felt good.

As good as the crisp air hitting her cheeks today when Colin opened the screen door, still chewing on his toast but eager to get outside.

She could hear Lyndsay fussing at him from down the hall.

"Are you sure you don't want a jacket, Colin? I know it's May, but . . ."

"Maria and I are going to be gardening," Colin protested. "I won't need it."

Maria wasn't sure why they even used gardening as their excuse anymore. It was quite obvious that their sorry little patch had stayed more or less the same, apart from a few half-hearted weeding expeditions and some of the straggly plants left over from their actual plot that Colin occasionally dragged the hose over to and doused while they discussed their next plans.

Lyndsay didn't seem to mind. She seemed content with encountering them lolling on the lawn, or their expeditions up the street to "research" with Rick and Mimi.

Charlotte seemed a little more suspicious, but she was too caught up in her "spring cleaning" renovation plans for the upper floor of the house to sniff about it too often.

"Maria, you were sniffling yesterday. You aren't going outside without a hat over your scarf."

"It gives me a headache," Maria insisted, but only half-heartedly. Secretly, she didn't mind it when Lyndsay came over to fuss with her hat, tugging it down and then raising it back up.

Lyndsay's fingers lingered to push Maria's flyaway curls back under the cloth and button up the top of her jacket. For a moment she paused, even though she'd done everything she said she needed to do.

And, for some reason, Maria didn't want to push her away.

"Have fun out there," Lyndsay said. She didn't quite smile, but Maria could see it in her eyes.

It was weird how that expression used to unnerve her, but now it was like seeing the sun come out.

"We will," Maria said.

Colin didn't look at her, putting his violin case over his shoulder. But even though he didn't respond to Lyndsay, Maria noticed that he grabbed his jacket on the way out.

"So now we have a good layout for the new plants we're putting in," Colin said as they walked down the familiar path.

It was springier under their feet than it had been in late March when she first found the garden: bright and green and still damp with morning dew.

"Are we doing peppers today?"

"I think so," Maria replied. "Mimi and Rick should be bringing them later."

Dadima was giving them some of her own store: bright and green and already half grown.

"I think I can trust you all with this," she had said with a smile. "At least, as long as you let Maria tend to them. She does have that magic touch, it seems."

Maria liked the sound of that.

Maria's magic.

It was like she had a talent, as much as Rick had his knack

with animals and bugs and Mimi was apparently an artist and Colin had his music.

"Here you go."

Colin held the gate open for Maria to pass.

The nearest patch to the gate was still waiting as they had left it the previous night, a bag of mulch on its side where Mimi and Rick had breathlessly let it drop. Another bounty from their dadima's supply.

They silently pulled on their gloves and then set to work, spreading more of the mulch and patting it over the layer of weeded soil they'd worked so hard to free. Maria paused a few times to close her eyes and relish the rich, woody smell taking root in her nose.

Paired with the sunshine drenching them, it was so comforting that she wished she could take root in the patch herself. Hopefully the plants felt that way too.

As the morning sun rose higher in the sky, they stepped back from their efforts.

Colin turned to Maria.

"Mind if I practice? I looked up some coping things I could do to not feel so overwhelmed by the speed of it, and I want to try."

They worked their way back to the bench, and Maria took a seat, making sure not to nudge the old CD player balancing on the edge next to the faded sari. It had been a gift from Mimi a few nights before.

"Dadima said Colin's mom liked music when she was out here," she said, beaming from ear to ear as she always did. "I thought it might be nice to keep up that tradition."

The CDs were full of old Bengali pop, songs Maria recognized from her own mom's favorites. It both soothed her and made her heart ache. She was relieved that Colin wanted to practice his piece, and that the CD player wouldn't be turned on yet.

Colin put his violin under his chin.

He looked anxiously toward Maria.

"It's okay," she said. "Just . . . try."

"I know," he muttered. Another deep breath, and then he lowered his bow to the strings.

And it flew.

The music truly reminded Maria of the bumblebee for which it was named: dizzily spinning through the air, wildly finding its way from bloom to bloom, and eventually staggering under the weight of the pollen its legs gathered.

It was amazing.

Colin was amazing.

As he held the last note, Maria saw a flutter out of the corner of her eye. She felt—no, she knew—what it was before she turned her head: the little brave piece of sari, fluttering in the wind.

Colin's mom was cheering him on.

And when Colin lowered his bow, face sweaty, Maria stood up and clapped with her.

"Did I do it?" Colin gasped.

"It sounded to me like you did," Maria said, not even thinking to add her usual biting commentary to it. "You did it, Colin."

Colin let his violin fall to his side, beaming, mouth opening to say something—and then he froze.

Maria turned, following his gaze.

And her stomach plummeted.

At the gate, breathless and clutching her jacket closed at the neck, was Lyndsay Clayborne.

XIV ❧ *Crushed Underfoot*

Like a cup pushed off a counter

like a scoop of ice cream under a ray of sun

like a foot skating off a puddle on slick tile

> Maria is unsettled
> and then
> upended
> and then
> undone.

Like a ripe fruit dropping from a branch

like a bent nail caught in a door

like a carton of eggs sliding from a plastic bag

> Maria's stomach nosedives to her toes.
> Maria's heart splatters against her ribs.
> Maria's tongue glues to the roof of her mouth.

It is sickening to be on the other end of the accident

      to be the cup rather than the clumsy hand

      to be the melting, miserable aftermath

          of a sweet, tantalizing possibility

    to know exactly how it feels

      to be the green, hopeful seedling

      to raise your head with no expectations for

anything except

          light

          air

          growth

          hope

  and

      then

          comes down

            the foot.

Twenty-Five

All Maria could do was stand there.

The sun should recede behind clouds, the birds should stop chirping, the whole world should be as sick and shocked and upended as her stomach. But around them, the garden continued to teem. With a slight tickle, the tik-tiki crawled up her leg and slid into her pocket.

Lyndsay gripped the iron of the gate in the same way someone might seek out the railing on a set of stairs for balance.

"What are you two doing?"

"What does it look like we're doing?" Colin's voice was wobbly, but he held his head up as he stared at Lyndsay.

"Excuse me?" Lyndsay's voice went shrill. "Is this a joke to you? You've . . ."

At a loss for words, she flailed her hand around.

Maria craned her head, trying to see the garden through Lyndsay's eyes, to understand what made it so awful.

But she couldn't.

Because it was sunny, and bright, and taken care of now.

It was beautiful.

Yet Lyndsay was looking around like they'd ruined everything by making a garden exactly what it should be: a place where things bloomed.

Maria had thought she'd finally started to understand Lyndsay. Or maybe Lyndsay had started to understand them. She, Maria Latif, had actually put her faith in a grown-up.

Why had she done that?

"Colin, you know better than to break the rules, *again*, and get yourself in trouble. You know that lock was there for a reason."

Lyndsay's lips were so thin, they were a faint pink line on her bloodless face.

Maria clenched her fists. "It wasn't his idea. It was mine. And we weren't breaking the rules. I got permission, from Mr. Clayborne, to garden, didn't I?"

"You know he didn't mean this place," Lyndsay said, shaking her head. "Now how am I going to explain this, on top of everything else?"

Colin's eyes were fixed on something in Lyndsay's hand: a square of crumpled paper. For all Maria knew, it could be a recipe she had been holding when she rushed out to find them for . . .

Wait. Lyndsay had rushed out to find them. Why?

Colin seemed to know. He snarled, lunging forward at Lyndsay.

"Wait, that's . . . you went into my room? You can't do that!"

"I didn't," Lyndsay said tightly. "Your grandmother did, because apparently this letter was sent to us weeks ago and the director of the conservatory called your father, worried, because he hadn't heard back from me on the status of your temporary leave and was wondering when you would be back at school. Imagine our surprise at hearing the words 'temporary leave.'"

"Dad . . . Dad called here? What did he say? What did you tell him?" Colin asked, his voice trembling.

Lyndsay stared at him. "Colin! What were you thinking? That they wouldn't follow up with us at all if we never sent you back? That you could just hang around forever? What is going on with you?"

The fight felt like something Maria shouldn't be part of. When they finally realized she was still there, it was going to get worse. But she couldn't move.

"It wasn't your business," Colin snapped.

"What happens in this house is my business just as much as yours. And believe it or not, I poke into your business because I care about you, Colin Clayborne."

Colin laughed harshly. "Yeah, right. You're not my mom, Lyndsay. And you're *not* a Clayborne. Stop acting like one."

There were many times in her short, grumpy life that Maria had allowed herself to unleash the words that formed like bitter, ill-shaped pearls under her tongue, letting them spill into the extended hands of the adults around her: thoughts about them, and their irritating kids.

She hadn't felt guilty about those words, ever.

(Not that she would admit.)

But even though she hadn't said these particular words, they fell like a weight against her own heart: *How could you say that?*

Why would you say that?

Lyndsay looked like she'd been slapped. For a moment, they all stood in the thick silence.

"Okay," Lyndsay said, her voice quavering. "Fine. You win, Colin. You're right. I'm not your mom. I'm not a Clayborne."

Colin blinked hard, like he wanted to cry, but he kept his spine stiff and fists clenched.

Maria wasn't sure why she wanted to both hug him and smack him.

"So," Lyndsay continued, still in that strange, strained voice, "since I'm not either of those things, that means you're not my problem. Tomorrow you and your father can have a nice long talk about the garden and school and whatever else you're hiding."

Colin froze.

Maria's tongue felt swollen in her mouth. She had to clear her throat in order to force out the words. "Wait. Mr. Clayborne . . . is . . ."

"Coming back tomorrow," Lyndsay said wearily.

Colin bolted toward Lyndsay. She flinched, actually throwing up her hands, but Colin veered around her and ran out the gate.

Leaving the garden. Leaving Maria.

"Colin!" Maria called after him, stunned.

He didn't stop.

He didn't even turn.

Like she didn't matter.

"Let him go, Maria. Your turn now. Why?"

Lyndsay's voice was brittle as glass.

Maria balled her hands into fists at her sides, trying to
steady herself.

"We're taking care of it. The garden was dying and rotting.
It needed—wanted—someone to care. Why should I feel sorry
for that?"

Lyndsay massaged her temples. "It's not about being sorry
for caring, Maria. Colin is enough of a handful, but you . . .
don't you know . . ."

She trailed off.

But Maria could hear the end, loud and clear.

Colin was the son. He could skulk around in his room
and break the rules. They wouldn't ship him off, or make
urgent phone calls to place him in a new home that very night
because "We can't do this anymore."

They would never treat him the way they treated her.

That was what Lyndsay wanted to say: *Don't you know you
have everything to lose?*

"I do," Maria said, answering the unspoken question. She
wasn't sure why her voice was so creaky, why her palms itched
and her eyes stung.

She had been through this scene before. So why did it hurt
so much, going through it now with Lyndsay?

"Maria," Lyndsay started, reaching out.

Maria sidled back.

"I'm not sorry," Maria insisted. "So don't expect me to apologize. To you or Mr. Clayborne."

Lyndsay rubbed her arms and looked toward the gate. And then she spoke again.

"Go to your room."

Maria turned to her, eyes wide.

"What?"

"Go up to your room," Lyndsay said firmly. That anxious look she had had at the beginning of the conversation was back. "I'll close the gate, and see what I can do to . . . well, I'll close and lock it. But you can't come in here anymore."

Time to leave behind the dream.

Maria shook her head. No. It couldn't end this way.

"Why? We can ask permission from him tomorrow. We can . . ."

"Maria!"

There was no use telling Lyndsay about the garden's importance to Colin, or the tik-tiki that lived in its newly green depths, or how content the house had felt recently when she stepped in with dirt still clinging to the bottoms of her bare feet after several blissful hours of shoeless wandering.

Not when Lyndsay had already shut herself away as firmly as she did her own dreams.

So Maria pulled on the deepest, darkest parts of her heart.

"Okay, fine," she said, voice cold. "Send me away like you're so ready to. I'll be packing."

Before Lyndsay could reply, she swept past her to the house.

And once she got to her bedroom, she slammed the door. Hard.

Twenty-Six

In the movies, it always looked like some important point was made once you stormed off.

Behind you, the grown-up shook their head, regretting what they had said and preparing to offer some sob-fest speech about how wrong they were.

Maria stood just inside her room and waited . . . for something. For Colin to remember her, and creep back down from his room so they could figure out what to do.

For Lyndsay to bring one of those tentative, apologetic smiles alongside a plateful of Dadima's goodies: curried pumpkin spooned over rice with mashed egg bhorta on the side, or maybe a stray rasmalai ball bursting with unspoken sweetness.

For the ringing in her ears and the pounding of her heart to stop, so she could think.

But nothing did happen.

There was silence.

Stillness.

Usually, this was what Maria wanted.

Usually, she would be proud. She hadn't taken Lyndsay's scolding with a ducked head, lip between her teeth.

Maria was never sorry, not when she was right.

And she was right, wasn't she?

So why was her stomach sour, like the day after she'd eaten too many underripe mangoes? Heart heavy, like she'd done something wrong? The silence stifling, instead of soothing and comforting?

It was the type of quiet that reminded Maria of when she was younger, and her parents weren't there. There was only an aunt and uncle who tried a little too hard and spoke a little too softly and played the saddest ghazals on the radio, tragic love songs that throbbed as painfully as a toothache.

She looked around the room. The torn pants Mimi was teaching her to mend were still strewn over the messy, sliding-off-the-bed duvet. The little bookshelf Lyndsay had dragged in for her still had the stack of gardening books from Dadima atop it, and one of the little potted plants that she had rescued after the cold snap.

The sight of it all was so homey that Maria couldn't stand it.

With a snarl, she tossed the pants off the bed. The needle clicked off and bounced over the floorboards. She kicked the side of the bookshelf, the books thumping and the potted plant crashing to the floor.

She could feel the house holding its breath, unsure of what to do with her, what warmth to soothe her with.

It wasn't the only one.

There was no stir from downstairs, no raising of Lyndsay's voice: "Maria? Are you okay up there?"

Of course there wouldn't be. Now she knew that Lyndsay, just like everyone else, was eager to get meddlesome, disrespectful, troublemaking Maria Latif off her hands.

Lyndsay was probably holed up in her kitchen, oversalting her rice or boiling brussels sprouts or making a disgusting *casserole* for lunch just because Charlotte wanted it. Maria hoped she was wincing as she swallowed a little to see if it was overcooked enough to be slimy and tasteless.

Maria slowly slid down the wall and tucked her knees up under her. She closed her eyes and inhaled. It was such a babyish thing to do. The smell of rosewater and milk-steeped sweets, warm tea and fresh bread seeped from the walls, and the floorboards hummed with tunes from the old radio hundreds of miles and a whole life away.

She could almost feel her mother's long, gentle fingers weaving oil and warm, hushed bedtime stories into her hair. She could almost hear her father in his office, singing religious praises or proud freedom songs older than any of them.

But she knew when she opened her eyes, nothing would have changed.

Her parents would still be dead.

She would still be sent away again.

She would have to leave this room, and this house, and her friends, and her garden.

The tik-tiki crawled out of her pocket and tickled her leg as it climbed her knee. As she looked at its little green body, it blurred. She was crying.

She cried for the garden. For all the plants she had brought back to life, had given a second chance.

She cried for Colin, and for Colin's mother, who had left behind saris and soil because she couldn't stay herself.

She even cried for Lyndsay, who had looked just as out of place as Maria at first, but had finally made at least the kitchen her own, and who she had thought understood her through all the smiles and shared recipes and tea.

She cried for Mimi, and Rick, because they were kind and

warm, even if they were loud and annoying too.

She cried for the little tik-tiki, who would be left all alone without a pocket to curl up in.

And then she cried for herself.

The girl who got shuffled from house to house so often she couldn't feel the bumps in the road any more than her suitcase.

The girl who was always placed by the door, so it would be easier for her to leave.

The girl who had, despite herself, put down roots: little soft, feathery, delicate ones that had found tilled earth where they expected hard-set soil (Lyndsay's hand on her shoulder, Colin's shy smile, Mimi and Rick's dadima patting her cheek). Despite every rule she made about dealing with adults and new houses, she had expected to stay.

But when you were Maria Latif, that wasn't something you were allowed to do—expect anything.

Or, well, expect anything *good*.

She had forgotten that.

And now she was crying. She *hated* crying.

"Ugh," Maria muttered. Her whole face felt like a mess of snot and tears. "Gross."

She needed to stop being such a *baby*. It wasn't going to help anything, anyway.

Maria sniffed again, and looked at the mess she'd made of the room.

With a sinking heart, she took in the potted plant lying on its side. Thankfully, it wasn't broken. Maria sighed in relief. Soil had spilled out, and she grimaced as she swept it back in and righted the pot.

Her hand connected with something she didn't expect. Something soft, and fuzzy.

Maria gasped and leaned down closely. It was a sprout!

A whole, leafy carrot seedling. She took a breath.

And the garden rose up to meet her: freshly unfurled flower blooms, the spicy underside of a leaf, the stubborn clang of iron from old tools, and most importantly, the earth.

Her bit of earth, turned over and crumbling through her fingers: deep and beautifully brown and as rich smelling as a chocolate cake, in the weirdest way.

Good and new and ready to bite into.

Maria looked down at the seedling and felt the hateful sting of tears in the corner of her eyes again.

"I wasn't wrong," she whispered.

The plant hadn't died in the frost after all. She wasn't wrong to believe it needed another chance. She wasn't fooling herself, thinking that the garden needed her. And she couldn't leave without putting up a fight.

She held the pot to her chest. She'd have to talk to Colin before Mr. Clayborne arrived. They needed to stand up for the garden together. They needed to stand up for each other.

Maria scrambled up, fumbling for her fallen dupatta, but froze at a knock on her door.

Could it be Lyndsay? She wasn't sure if she was ready for that conversation, not now.

But then she heard a whisper. "Maria! Maria, are you in there?"

"Colin?"

Without hesitation, Maria yanked the door open. There he was, looking even worse than she must. His face was puffy, his hair stuck up on one side, and his eyes were very red.

Under her stare, he flushed.

"I got something in them," he started, but Maria shook her head.

"Forget it. Look, we need to talk."

Colin shushed her, pulling on her arm. "Come downstairs. No, wait, grab your suitcase first. Hurry!"

"Colin, what . . ."

Before she could say anything more, Colin had reached past her for the suitcase himself. Not even seeming to notice it was empty, he grabbed it and made down the stairs.

Exasperated, Maria followed him, hesitating when he pushed open the kitchen door.

"Lyndsay's upstairs cleaning the bedroom or something," Colin said. "Listen, I've been thinking and thinking about this. I shouldn't have stormed off and left you to face Lyndsay on your own. I thought I would be able to talk to you at lunch, but you didn't come."

"You went back down after *that*?"

"I was hungry! Is that a crime?"

Maria sighed and shook her head. "Okay, so what were you thinking so hard about?"

Colin swallowed. "Let's run away."

Twenty-Seven

"Run away?"

Maria gaped at Colin in disbelief.

"Not so loud," Colin hissed, looking over his shoulder anxiously. "Look, I thought Lyndsay would take my phone, but she didn't bother. I found two bus tickets back upstate online, and I emailed my adviser to see exactly what they talked about after she found the letter—"

"Seriously," Maria broke in. "Under your pillow? What were you thinking?"

"I'm sorry, okay?" Colin threw his hands up in the air. "I'm not good at figuring out places to hide things. I panicked!"

"Rolled up in a pair of socks. Beneath your mattress. In an empty bedpost," Maria listed flatly. "In the bulb of your lamp—just say it blew out and you need to replace it."

Colin stared at her. "How do . . . forget it. I don't want to know. Anyway. My adviser said that she definitely needs to have a conversation with my dad and me and Lyndsay about moving forward with a diagnosis and a support plan, but she *did* say that I'm still welcome back. You can come with me. We'll convince her, somehow."

Colin's eyes were red, the hand on his precious violin case so tight that his knuckles were white.

Over his shoulder was slung a half-zipped backpack.

She could see a white T-shirt sticking out, and a toothbrush, and . . . was that sheet music?

He was serious.

"Colin, what are you doing?" She pulled the backpack off his shoulder and set it down on the floor with a thump. "Give me that."

Colin held on firmly to his violin case. "Stop that."

"No. You stop it. Okay? Colin, I've been bouncing around relatives' houses for a year." Maria swallowed hard. "At first, it would be okay, but then . . . they would realize that this was for real. It wasn't just a visit. They had a grumpy, unpleasant orphan to deal with. I wasn't a guest anymore. I was a problem."

Colin's face creased, and he reached out toward her.

"Maria. You're not a problem."

"I am, and it's okay," Maria said sharply. "It's not like I got this way because my parents died. People lose their parents all the time, right? And apparently they just keep smiling through it and saying yes to whatever the grown-ups decide. And I'm not like that."

"But you shouldn't have to be," Colin insisted, grasping her shoulders. "And you shouldn't have to be okay with it. You shouldn't have to smile."

Colin Clayborne, of all people, was trying to comfort her.

And her eyes were prickling and her throat was closing up like some big baby.

It was silly. So silly.

It shouldn't be a big deal.

"Anyway," she forced out, reaching up to rub her sleeves across her eyes—just because the itching was getting to her, that was all. "That's not the point. The point is, I'm staying here. I may not be getting my home back, but I can stay right here. And so should you."

Colin recoiled, dropping his hands, but Maria pushed on.

"Look, Colin. It won't work and you know it. Sooner or later, you're going to have to face your dad. Running away puts that off, but it doesn't fix it."

As weird as it was to be so attached to this boy who only

seemed to complicate her life, she didn't want him to run away when he could fight for himself.

At least one of them had a parent left, and a home. A place, not just a temporary space.

Colin sighed harshly and pushed a hand through his hair.

"Okay. Look. You're right. I know you're right, but . . ."

The next words he spoke were so low, Maria had to lean forward to hear.

"From the moment I was born, it's felt like my dad has just seen me as a Clayborne, and never as Colin. Everything I do is wrong. Everything. I could drop a plate while unloading the dishwasher, and he'd tell me that Ma would be so disappointed in me. Even school wasn't an escape from it. It felt like every teacher was judging me, waiting to report back to him. So I gave them something else to talk about first. The guy I shoved mouthed off at me about something, and usually I would let it go. But all I could think about was, *Dad will be disappointed, but I won't have to talk about the other stuff.*"

Colin looked up, his eyes brimming with tears.

Maria shuffled awkwardly. Seeing Colin cry was almost as bad as crying herself. They were the grumpy, prickly kids. Not the ones who had emotional conversations in the middle of Lyndsay's kitchen in their stocking feet.

"I didn't care. I didn't care when I left school. I didn't care when I got here, but . . . the garden . . ."

Colin's shoulders shook.

"I don't want to hear him say anything bad about it," he choked out. "Not about me being out there. Not about what we planted, or the work we did. Or you. I can take it if he yells at me. I'm used to it. But if he says anything to you . . ."

"Colin," Maria managed around the lump in her throat. That was all she could say.

No one worried about her like this.

Not since her parents.

Colin looked down at his feet, and Maria looked over his head at the little cow timer on the counter.

It stared back.

Underneath her feet, the floorboards creaked.

And warmed.

When she drew in a breath, it was scented with notes of sugared chai, fresh bread, and blooming flowers.

Home. Family. Warmth.

That was what Colin was to her. And that was what she wanted to be to him.

Maria reached out and closed her hand over Colin's.

He looked up. His nose was snotty, and his face pinched

and thin, like when she had first met him. Back then, she'd thought he was an awful-looking boy—but now, for some reason, the sight of him gave her a weird, squirmy feeling in her chest.

"Colin," Maria said, as gently as it was possible for Maria Latif to be. "We can't run away."

"I have fifty dollars," Colin insisted stubbornly. "I can take care of you. So you don't need to worry."

Maria sniffed, mainly because—as she well knew from the many aunties she had been raised by—it was a good way to hide how touched she was.

And then she reached out and shoved him.

"Are we in a Bollywood movie or something? Get a grip. What do you expect me to do, live in a garbage can like Oscar the Grump or whatever his name is?"

"The Grouch?"

"Whatever. We're not leaving, so it doesn't matter."

Maria stamped her foot. She hadn't stamped it in so long, and it felt good. Colin just . . . he made her so angry. He couldn't be scared now. She wouldn't let him.

"That isn't your father's garden, Colin Clayborne. It's yours. And mine, and Mimi and Rick's. We saved it. So if you give up now . . ."

Maria jutted her chin out. Her fists shook. That was good.

Angry Maria knew her strength, and how to make change with it.

"I'll . . . I'll never talk to you again. Ever. Even when we grow up. You can just stay here and mope with your violin and rot with the plants, and I won't even *care*."

Colin's eyes were as wide as dinner plates. For a moment, there was no sound in the kitchen: only Maria's angry breathing and the faint click of the clock on the wall ticking away the minutes.

One . . .

Two . . .

Three . . .

As the silence pressed in, Maria's anger bled away. Had she said too much?

What if Colin didn't care that she might be shipped away, never to see him or their plants or . . . or Lyndsay, even, again?

Colin's violin case thumped to the ground. Maria looked up.

Colin still looked pale. But his face was determined.

"Okay. So what do we do?"

And then they both jumped at a sound from outside: a firm, heavy thud.

A car door.

"Did you hear that?" Colin whispered.

"I heard something," Maria whispered back.

They both froze at the sound of the side gate scraping.

"Someone's going into the yard," Colin breathed. "It can't be . . ."

But Maria was already scrambling past him, not even bothering with her shoes. She hurtled down the dark back hallway, Colin on her heels, and out the door into the early afternoon light.

The estate sprawled before them: greenhouse gleaming, the little decoy garden tucked at its side, and farther down the path leading toward the garden was a dark figure.

An adult, walking quickly.

"Oh, that's cold," Colin gasped, wincing as his bare feet met the dewy grass.

"Never mind," Maria said. "Someone's headed for the garden. Come on!"

She flew down the path, toward the familiar iron gate . . . and lurched to a stop. Colin nearly collided with her back.

The gate was ajar.

She heard the click of the old CD player they had left by the plants, and the high-pitched hum of a Bengali love song washed out through the open gate.

Behind her, Colin's breath caught, and when he spoke, his

voice was odd and strained. "Maria, wait! Stop! I know who it is . . ."

Maria balled up her fists and barged forward.

But once inside, she froze.

Because she saw for herself who it was.

A tall, long beanpole of a man, wearing a wrinkled suit, glasses perched haphazardly on his head. He was crouched near the CD player, peering curiously at the seedlings.

Maria had only seen him in pictures. He looked older—sadder, with a scruffy beard over his chin.

But that chin was Colin's chin.

Those gloomy eyes were Colin's eyes.

"Dad," Colin whispered, stopping behind Maria.

Mr. Clayborne rose to his feet and looked at the two of them.

"Well," he said. "Hello."

Twenty-Eight

It wasn't until this moment Maria realized that, despite everything Colin and Lyndsay had said, she had expected to like Mr. Clayborne instantly, the way kids always seemed to like the mysterious adopted father in movies.

Maria had never been the cheery Hollywood orphan type. She knew that better than anyone else. But she had still wondered if something might kick in at some point. It was a relief to know that, at heart, she was still Maria Latif, who made quick and firm opinions for herself and judged adults the way she wanted to, not the way anyone expected her to.

"Maria," Mr. Clayborne said. He said it slowly, as though weighing it out and making sure it suited her. "You look like your parents. Have you heard that before?"

"Yes," Maria said.

She knew it wasn't true. She would have preferred if he said something about the dirt under her nails, or the little mole to the side of her nose, or the forthrightness of her stare.

The things that made her Maria.

"Dad. How did you . . . ," Colin started from behind her. "Where did you . . ."

For the first time, Mr. Clayborne looked at him.

"I was able to get an earlier flight, after I spoke with Lyndsay," Mr. Clayborne said. He tilted his head and looked at his son for a long moment. "She didn't mention anything at all about this."

"She didn't know," Colin mumbled. "Sir."

Sir?

It sounded so distant, so fearful, like a prisoner addressing his jailer.

"I see," was all Mr. Clayborne said.

Maria and Colin exchanged glances. Maria wasn't sure how her face looked, but her tongue stuck to the roof of her mouth. Colin was deathly pale.

Mr. Clayborne sighed heavily and shook his head. "I shouldn't be as impressed with all this as I am right now."

"What?" Colin blurted out. Maria couldn't blame him.

He was . . . impressed?

Mr. Clayborne turned toward the bench.

"I had a dream on the plane," he said, "about something impossible."

He stared down at the sari that Maria had left untouched, keeping its tight hold on one rusted handle.

"Saira," Mr. Clayborne breathed. It was the softest, most gentle, his voice had been. "I had a dream that she was waiting here for me."

He reached out to touch the sari, but before his fingertips could touch the cloth, it reared up and arced back in a sudden breeze.

Maria jumped, and Colin gasped beside her.

Mr. Clayborne clenched his hand in the air for a moment. And then he turned back to face Maria and Colin.

"She was waiting, in her garden, with all the flowers in bloom," he said. "For the first few years after she died, I couldn't bear to come in here. And then, when I tried to revive it, nothing I did worked. So I locked it up and tried to forget about it. Until this dream, where it was blooming just like before. Even though I knew it was impossible, I couldn't shake it off."

He looked over at Maria. "I have something for you."

He pulled his wallet from his pocket and fumbled through it for a moment. Then he held a folded paper out to Maria.

She eyed it warily before taking it. A present for her?

When Maria unfolded the paper, her entire body froze.

Colin leaned over her shoulder and sucked in a breath.

"Maria, are those . . ."

"My parents," Maria said through the sudden lump in her throat. There they were, in a crumpled, faded photograph, but still shimmering brightly.

Perfect, gleaming stars.

And there was someone else too, leaning up against her mother's side, more wan but with just as warm a smile.

"My mom," Colin breathed, reaching out a trembling fingertip to touch his mother's face. "And . . ."

"And you," Maria realized, looking at the grouchy little toddler clasped protectively in those thin arms. "Baby you!"

"You too," Mr. Clayborne interjected.

His shadow fell over Colin's mother's face as he leaned in, pointing to Maria's mother's lap. Yes, she was there too: a bundle in the crook of her mother's arms. Even that small, Maria was sure she could see a little pout on her lips, a little frown on her face.

Yet that was where her parents' gazes were turned, rays of sunlight warming their grumpy, prickly, unpleasant baby.

Their Maria.

The star that completed their constellation.

Maria's eyes stung. She blinked back the tears and focused on the background of the photo. It was the garden at her parents' house, and for the first time, Maria realized how similar it was to *this* garden.

"These plants," she said, finally looking back up at Mr. Clayborne. "Are they . . ."

Mr. Clayborne gave a shadow of a smile.

"Saira and your mother were always trading gardening tips. They visited us before you two were born, and then after, when we visited you, Saira laughed at how your mother had copied her garden. That was the last time she saw them."

"Maybe that's why you found this garden, Maria," Colin said.

She looked at him, and then looked around at the neat little sprouts and the tools still strewn about on the ground. Maybe he was right. Maybe that was how she had sensed what was meant to grow here.

Maybe that was why this garden felt like . . . home.

Mr. Clayborne cleared his throat.

"I'm surprised, Colin," Mr. Clayborne said. "To see you so interested in the outdoors."

"Well," Colin fumbled, raising his hand to the back of his neck. "I . . . I wanted to help Maria, and . . ."

"I see. That's . . . that's actually kind."

Maria didn't like the look on his face, or the way that he said it: like he both meant it, and didn't. Like he didn't really believe that his son could be kind.

It was the same look Asra had given her, as if a Maria who could wander around outside and not be a problem was a Maria she had never believed could exist.

"It was his mom's garden," Maria burst out. "Why would it be a surprise? She brought him out here all the time."

"Maria," Colin hissed, but Mr. Clayborne just sighed.

"Yes. She did, didn't she? Maybe I've done too much forgetting."

Maria waited for more. But he was quiet.

"Sir," Colin burst out suddenly. "About the leave from school . . ."

Mr. Clayborne's eyes focused. "Yes. To be honest, I had a whole speech prepared for you, and I don't even know what to say now."

Colin bit his lip.

"Sir . . ."

"We talked about this, and all I can say is that I'm very, very disappointed. I really thought, after the last time, it was going better. You were doing better."

Mr. Clayborne shook his head. He wasn't even saying it in an angry way. Just a tired, unsurprised way.

"You know your mother would expect you to at least try. I don't think that's too much to ask."

Maria stared at Colin incredulously, her hands balled into fists. How could his father tell him he wasn't trying, when it was all he did every day?

Defend yourself! Say something!

But Colin didn't.

Instead, another voice broke in.

"How dare you treat your own son this way?"

Colin and Maria whirled around. It couldn't be.

"Lyndsay?"

It was indeed Lyndsay Clayborne, arms folded and lips turned down in a disappointed frown. But unlike this morning, it wasn't directed at Colin and Maria.

Her eyes were fixed on her husband.

Twenty-Nine

Mr. Clayborne stared at Lyndsay as though he'd never seen her before in his life.

And Maria could see why.

Lyndsay had color to her cheeks. When she folded her arms, there was a flash of sunshine-yellow turmeric on her fingers— likely from her recent ventures into different types of curry. The henna in her hair shimmered in the afternoon light.

Mr. Clayborne didn't take his eyes off her, even as his mother appeared behind her.

"Ethan!" Charlotte said. "We were expecting you tomorrow. What . . ."

Lyndsay held Mr. Clayborne's gaze. "What were you just saying to Colin?" she asked, voice firm.

Charlotte turned a disapproving stare on Lyndsay. "Lyndsay, how can you—"

"Charlotte," Lyndsay said, in a tone that made Charlotte sputter. "I'm talking, please."

Mr. Clayborne tugged on his tie and took a step forward.

"I was trying to get to the bottom of Colin's latest escapade."

Colin's mouth worked. "I . . . I was having a hard time," he started. "I needed . . . I just wanted . . ."

Mr. Clayborne let out a short, harsh laugh. "A hard time? I have a hard time too, Colin, but I don't decide to run away."

Yes, you do.

Maria gritted her teeth.

Why else had he been gone so long? Why else did he keep the garden locked? Why, even now, was he not looking his own son in the eye?

"Yes, you do," Lyndsay said. Her prickly tone of voice prodded goose bumps up Maria's arms. Lyndsay, actually thinking the same things Maria did!

Lyndsay seemed shocked with herself. But the words kept coming.

"This hasn't been an easy time for any of us. But not because of Colin. Yes, he has been . . ." She looked at Colin, and shrugged. "He's been a challenge. But in the past month, I've finally gotten to know him. And I realized his anger wasn't because of me, but you. Everything you've ignored."

Colin looked utterly astonished. Lyndsay stepped forward and put her arm around him.

"He's not a disappointment, Ethan," she said. "He's a boy who is trying his best. That's all he can do."

"Thanks, Lyndsay," Colin said in a watery voice. His shoulders heaved.

"Oh, Colin," Charlotte breathed. For the first time, she looked old, and very tired. "Don't cry."

Colin's head yanked up, his eyes red, his cheeks streaked with tears.

"Why? Because a Clayborne doesn't do that?" He glared at Charlotte, and then Mr. Clayborne. "Well, maybe we should be able to cry. Maybe then we could finally talk about Mom. I miss her too, you know. And I barely even know her! Because you don't let me."

Mr. Clayborne looked at Colin, his face drawn.

"Colin," he said, in a quiet voice. "I don't want to be the bad guy from some fairy tale and hide your mother from you. But losing her was very hard for me, and it took me a long time to come to terms with the fact that she wasn't coming back. It still hurts to talk about—"

"Can't you understand your grief isn't the only hurt on the table, Ethan?" Lyndsay interrupted, her face ablaze. "I don't think you ever did get over Saira's death. You simply locked it away—just like this garden. You didn't think about what other people needed to heal. You didn't think about your son. Colin deserves to know his mother."

Mr. Clayborne turned away, unable to meet Lyndsay's fierce gaze.

"I deserve to be loved too," Lyndsay continued. "I tried so hard to be a Clayborne that I forgot what it meant to be Lyndsay, or even to miss being myself. It wasn't until Maria started coming in and poking at my recipes that I realized what was missing: my own self. *My* taste for food. *My* family recipes."

Maria couldn't believe what she was hearing. Had she really been that much of an inspiration for Lyndsay?

Her, a grumpy, prickly kid?

"And what about Maria? She's going through the same loss as Colin, and everyone seems to think she's just fine with being shipped here and sent there. Like she's a package instead of a kid who needs to be cared for. Even you invited her, and then left. Can you imagine how that must have *felt*?"

Maria's cheeks prickled, and so did her eyes. Beside her, Colin timidly grasped her hand.

Lyndsay *knew.* Somehow she knew that even though Maria

acted like all the moving around was simply an inconvenience, deep inside, she was sad.

And lonely.

And really, really wanted her mom and dad.

And hadn't found the best way to go on without them. Until the garden.

"Your wife is right," Charlotte spoke. "You have been running away all this time, and I've let you. It's time to stop."

She stepped between Mr. Clayborne and the rest of them. "You may recall that before this was Saira's garden, it was mine. But Saira made it truly thrive. I should never have let you lock it up. I was too obsessed with it being the Clayborne way: turning our heads, not letting ourselves feel, ignoring the past. But maybe it was waiting for Maria to see it as it should be. Maybe the Clayborne way isn't the only way things should be."

Maria was stunned. Kind words for her, from Charlotte?

"Whoa," Colin whispered. "Grandma really said . . . it's okay to not do it the Clayborne way."

Mr. Clayborne looked around the garden. "You're right," he said softly. "Saira's garden. And now Maria's. I missed a lot. I missed a lot of things."

"It's not just my garden."

Maria's voice burst out before she even realized it. Mr.

Clayborne and Lyndsay both turned to her, and Charlotte jumped a little.

"What?" Mr. Clayborne asked.

"Well, at first I wanted it to be my garden," Maria continued.

Her voice was trembling. She had the terrible suspicion that she was going to do a very not-Maria Latif thing and cry, for the second time in a day. But if there was one thing Maria Latif had never done, it was shy away from saying what she wanted to say. And she wanted to say this.

No. She *needed* to say it.

"I was so sure I would be able to make it something incredible by myself. But . . ." Maria swallowed hard. "I was wrong. It could never be just mine, not when Colin is here. And Mimi and Rick too. This garden wasn't meant to be locked up. It was meant to be shared."

Mr. Clayborne wilted onto the bench. He was pale, his hand fluttering near his head as though he didn't know if he wanted to rub his chin or smooth down his hair. But he didn't say anything, so Maria continued.

"Look at what Mrs. Clayborne planted," Maria said. She bent down to touch a sprout. "Not pretty flowers, but pumpkin and squash that have flowers you can fry, and peppers and eggplant and okra. Plants that were home for her. And could be for Colin—even now that's she gone. And for you too."

Before Maria could say anything more, Lyndsay broke in. "She's right."

Maria looked up at her, surprised. Lyndsay's eyes were shimmering with tears.

"I stayed out here earlier, after I made the kids leave. Maria and Colin probably thought I was angry and I was going to tear things up. But I wasn't angry. I was scared."

That was the last thing Maria expected to hear. Lyndsay laughed softly.

"Yes, I was scared. I was scared of how mad Ethan was going to be, and how Charlotte was going to let me have it for upsetting him. But I was most scared because I didn't want you to get in trouble." She glanced at Colin. "Either of you."

Colin looked down at his feet. Maria wondered if he was thinking of all the times he had snapped at her. There was a lump rising in her throat. It hurt to look at Lyndsay's smile, but in a good way. The best way.

The way that makes you feel that you never want to look away from that face, from that person.

Lyndsay turned to Mr. Clayborne. "You know what I saw? A beautiful garden. That ugly gate was open and music was streaming out into the air, and the forsythia bushes were in bloom, their branches dangling over the fence like party garlands. I felt alive. I felt warm. I felt welcomed."

Lyndsay gave a little choked laugh.

"For the first time in this cold, unhappy house, I felt at home. Colin and Maria did that. For you—and for Colin's mother. And for me too."

Maria's eyes stung as she stared up into Lyndsay's kind face. She was still cupping the carrot sprout. She couldn't make herself move.

"So . . . ," she managed. "You aren't sending me away?"

"Maria Latif!" Lyndsay gasped. "Who told you I was sending you away? Wait, was it . . ."

She glared at Mr. Clayborne. Mr. Clayborne shuffled awkwardly.

"I didn't say a thing to her," he insisted.

"I always get sent away," Maria mumbled. "Every time. I'm too difficult. I talk back too much and I'm too prickly."

"But that's the way I like you," Lyndsay said softly. "I bet that's the way your parents liked you. And they knew their Maria best, even if they couldn't be here to see her bloom."

Maria gave a little watery hiccup.

"Maria." Lyndsay let go of Colin. She knelt on the earth beside her and grasped Maria's shoulders, looking her in the eyes.

"You are welcome with me, no matter what happens now. Kids are not packages you can send away when you're tired. Remember when I told you that you were your own person? I meant that. And I like the person Maria Latif is."

There was a pause before Charlotte shuffled forward and laid her hand on Maria's head.

"I do too," she said. And then sniffed. "Even if she gets into an awful lot of trouble."

Maria couldn't cry now.

Not over gushy moments like this.

You couldn't give adults that much power.

But when Lyndsay gathered her into a hug, she couldn't help it. Tears rolled down her cheeks.

And when Colin wrapped his arms around both her and Lyndsay, a little awkwardly, she let out the sob she was holding back.

"You will always have a home with me," Lyndsay continued. "Both of you. Okay?"

Maria could feel Colin's slow nod against the top of her head.

Right here, she felt at home.

Finally.

After a moment, Lyndsay cleared her throat and pulled away. Colin still grasped Maria's shoulders, and Maria darted